HORACE AND THE COIN

The adventures of Horace
Winterbottom in Australia

Gary John Carter

'On a world map of connections, we are all linked by roads of coincidence, six degrees of separation, and the chance of unexpected love.'

Acknowledgement

We are all just raindrops on the window of life, making our way to the river of knowledge. Some droplets race along and gain nothing, they are just drips. Others meander on the pane, growing, interacting, and gathering wisdom. They can create a flood through their attraction, and a storage dam of thoughts with their conversation. It was a splash to meet all the travellers, story tellers, and so many good people, on my window of life.

CONTENTS

FORWARD

The travel bug is better than a virus

Horace Winterbottom was a career journalist who came from the Cotswolds district of southern England. He was a true Englishman of the Winston Churchill ilk, and an avid William Shakespeare fan. He was born in Bourton-on-the-Water, which is considered '*the Venice of the Cotswolds.*' It is where Horace attended the Cotswold Grammar, his ticket to a good career. With just a toe into the Cornwall West country, he spoke with a restrained and slightly marbled Cornish accent. He still called a Car a Cor, and dropped the occasional H, but that was hardly noticeable in his refined voice.

In later life, as Horace approached that fourty-year-old milestone, he dressed like a funeral director. He loved his Derby Bowler hat. If he wore sunglasses he could be auditioning for a role in a '*Men in Black*' movie.

Horace did not have what some people might call movie star looks. He was more like a Ricky Gervais type than a George Clooney type, meaning he was snuggly, but not ugly. He played cricket and rugby at school, but was more suited to academia, although he did achieve a green belt in Judo at the age of twenty.

Horace stood 175cm tall, and lately supported a very slight beer related potbelly. He had few relationships in his life, and his neighbour and friend Beryl Fobsworth was always there. She had eyes for him, from their days at Cotswold Grammar, but Horace was never committed. He was one of those new age, *'stays-at-home-for-life,'* free loaders. Since his father passed, it was just him and his mum, so why move out. He was away most of the time anyway. One thing Horace loved about living in Bourton-on-the Water was Christmas. He explained to an enquiry in Australia once.

"When the snow falls there, you dress warm, walk through the village along the Windrush River, pass a succession of little stone bridges, and then have tea and scones at the Waterfront Tea Room. Afterwards you go back to your lodgings, grab your sled and head for the nearest high hill, like in the story of Rupert. It's only then that you know you're in the magic, that is the Cotswolds."

The last time he was in Australia was 2019. It was at the end of spring and as Australians say it, *'as dry as a dead dingo's donger.'* From the flight into Hobart, and a short stay in a haunted Salamanca 19th century house, he hired a car. He then visited, Port Arthur, Freycinet Peninsular, Cradle Mountain and the Tarkine wilderness. Sadly, he didn't find the now extinct Tasmanian Tiger, nor an extinct Tasmanian Aboriginal. 19th century clearing of land, animals, and humans, to allow room for sheep and apples, had Anglified the eastern half of the country. We were lucky that the Southwest corner didn't become the new state of Israel at the end of World War Two, as such, that area, and the Tarkine remain relatively untouched today.

In the past the pristine rivers made way for some Hydro dams and arguments. There were also many fights with the Greenies and the Loggers over old growth forests. Those fights still go on today, but when all the trees are gone there will be nothing left to fight over. Thankfully that won't include the dead and indestructible Huon pines which will last forever at the bottom of lakes and rivers. Horace perceived the problems, but still found it to be a beautiful place. He did note that the narrow roads and fast drivers provided plenty of roadkill for the iconic Tasmanian Devil, which for the moment hasn't become a memory.

During the last ice age, Tasmania was connected to the mainland. After the melt, twelve thousand years ago, all the locals were stranded, cold and probably happy until smallpox arrived. Tassie is now 250 kilometres from its mother, so Horace had to catch a ferry to Melbourne. He then travelled north on his south coast exploration from Melbourne to Sydney. When he crossed the border from Victoria to New South Wales near Mallacoota, he discovered the wonders of drought.

Horace stopped briefly at Eden, where he learnt about the cruelty man could inflict on whales in a by-gone age. It was here that Orca Whales herded Southern Right Whales into the harpoons of men. All for the price of a whale tongue. It was no Eden at that time for Horace either, climate change and associated rising temperatures had many people worried. The normal verdant green dairy country was a haystack just shy of a match or a lightning strike. This windy retirement kingdom of aging New South Welshmen and ladies was preparing for their own Armageddon. In the north from Queensland to Sydney, north westerly winds and fourty-degree days were causing fire storms.

Horace just made it back to Sydney before the roads were blocked. He flew back to London for a cold Christmas, the relief of a Cotswold doona, and loony lockdowns. The English Prime Minister, who needed a haircut, didn't go to Hawaii, he just stayed home during the Brexit fiasco and the many pandemic mistakes.

The 2019 Australian summer from hell hit the country hard. The aftermath of this tragedy saw thousands of square kilometres burnt out in many parts of Australia. Climate change had made such an impact that the bushfire smoke could be seen from space. People were killed and homes were destroyed, the wildlife suffered the most. The National parks were turned to cinders, littering the landscape with millions of animal corpses of birds, reptiles, and marsupials. In the end there was only a black brooding silence of misery. The fire fighters and volunteers had risked all and were hailed as heroes. The climate change denialist in the Federal Government were slow to act. Then, the Covid-19 pandemic struck with a force so strong that the entire world would feel it.

* * *

Horace had just returned to Sydney from England after a three-year hiatus, which had included the dreaded Covid-19 pandemic. He was lucky enough to get all his vaccinations, the only thing that got him was the travel bug. The blackened landscape of the East Coast was now awash with water. Floods were the new nightmare. The town of Lismore virtually disappeared under a sea of water, which was called the sky river. That was two years prior, and La Nina was intent on hanging around for a while longer. Horace was heading to the drier west on this adventure, and hopefully by the time he arrives back in Sydney, normality will have prevailed.

Horace was born with two qualities; they were facial recognition and charisma. The latter was like a magnet under a piece of paper. The human iron filings with their stories were attracted and gathered around him wherever he went. He was extremely observant of faces, although names were harder. His trade for the last twenty years was travel writing for the *'Finding Earth Magazine'*. In a typical English way, he had his faults, he was a biscuit dunker. On most occasions he managed to get the softened treat into his mouth before it splashed into the tea. It's funny the way English folk drink tea, with their little pinkie finger sticking out at a right angle to the cup, it may be for balance. His other favourite tipple was beer. Either cold or warm it didn't matter, so long as it was had with an enjoyable conversation.

In all his travels around the world, and especially it seems, in Australia, Horace had preconceived ideas of the nation's foibles. In major Australian capitals the first thing he notice were the plethora of real-estate posters. Real estate agents and funeral directors like to have their photographs on display. Horace had always been one for faces not names, so, as soon as he arrived somewhere, a hotel or a restaurant, he recognised people. Most of the time they were male real estate agents. For some unknown reason, perhaps because they like people to see their faces, or they feel that it is the only way their business can be known. With some, it may have been for vanity reasons. They believe their face sells the real-estate, not the premise. In most of the major cities Horace didn't need a face to pick a male real estate agent. They almost always wore dark blue suits with long sleeve cream shirts and pointy toed brown shoes with no socks. Generally, they would have a symbolic tie or a glary bow tie, like the ones Al Grassby, a Whitlam era politician would wear. He was known as the father of multiculturalism and audacious fashion. Horace had nothing against real estate agents or for that matter funeral directors, it was just something in his observations. He did note that the lady estate agents were always the pretty ones.

In Australia, Horace knew that the names of many of the Anglo-Celtics came from eighteenth century hanky and bread stealing convicts, or if you prefer, transports. The names were most likely recorded in the following fashion:

'Welcome to Port Jackson scumbags, there's a plough for you John Farmer, and your mate Tom Carter's brick cart is over by Mary Love's tent.'

He was also puzzled by the stuttered names of Australian towns, like Woy-Woy and Wagga-Wagga. He knew it had Aboriginal roots, yet there was no Manly-Manly or Dubbo Dubbo.

Horace would start his latest down-under journey from Sydney. The future plans were for an Indian Pacific rail excursion to Broken Hill, Adelaide, and Kalgoorlie. Then a few days learning about gold and the history of being thirsty. Then onward to Perth, where he would rent a car for a tour of the forests and sights of the southwest corner. He then intended to drive to Broome along the coast.

Horace had a few days to kill in Sydney before the train tour west, so he decided to ferry it to Manly, bus it through the wealthy peninsular to Palm Beach, then catch a ferry to Patonga for lunch. The ferries to Patonga were two hourly and with luck he would be having a cold beer and fish-n-chips at Patonga around noon.

CHARACTERS

Horace Winterbottom - A travel writer

Gwoya Jungarai - Our two-dollar coin Aboriginal

Marcus and Sally Canning - Tree House Café proprietors

Fiona Sharpe - Disgruntled lover serving prison time

Walter Shakeshaft - a Proctologist bard

Nancy Coogan - the voluptuous Kalgoorlie publican

Walkabout Jimmy and Likeable Billy - Pujari men

Morrice H Davidson - aka Mozzy - Great Aussie Blight

Lance Carbone - aka Boil - Sergeant at arms G.A.B

Ajax Rider - aka Jaxxy - biker G.A.B, had attitude to burn

Ethan Burlington - owner shark-dive boat off Cull Island

Hannah Fisher - a marine biologist from Perth

Mrs Gladys Trussell - Mum- dedicated wife Gracetown

Brian Trussell - Dad - Margaret River Cemetery, deceased

Trevor and Susan Trussell - animal shelter Oldbury W.A

Hu Chin - trader in exotic animals

Rizky Lestari - Boss of the animal trade syndicate

Gus Cook - Crab-Claw Café owner in Augusta

Chilli-Jam Johnson - aka Sultana-Bran - a country rocker

Bronwyn Tucker - Chilli's bird and groupie

Shane and Clarissa Huckster - Diamond smugglers

Tebogo Modise - Head of the Larona-pula syndicate

Zahi, Taifa & Axmed - aka the Lions of Mogadishu

Anne and Gayle Bagnall - Outback tour operators

Veronica Cullen - Chilli's new bird, owns a campervan

Waiehu Sakura - Japanese Marine Biology postgraduate

Doug Pitt - aka Digger, a miner from Broken Hill

Layla Pitt - aka flutter, a nurse from Orange

Tony Barber - Darwin storyteller, Antonio's Cuts barber

Iain Grieves - a Darwin funeral director

Gurigal Cudgegol - aka Plane Bob - Oenpelli Air pilot

Mugaroi Cudgegol - aka Capable Joe plane mechanic

Aunty Jill - the Injalak art - Yolngu people Gunbalanya

Isiah Couche - Brisbane psychiatrist, studies cults

Esmeralda Couche - wife and a Romani palm reader

Penelope weaver of charm - flautist cult lady

Cassandra who shines - flautist cult lady

Simon Song - aka Harmony cult leader Nimbin N.S.W

Shelby Wright -aka She'll be Right Mate-Deals on Wheels

Tom Howard - Deals on Wheels franchisee

Kyle and Linda Driver - Deals on Wheels franchisee

Scott Bannister - aka Scrags shallow end of the gene pool

Peter Simple - aka Pimple same pool but better looking

Reeya Lambros - a Greek girl Pimple likes

Sky Lovejoy - owner Lovejoy's Massage in Nimbin

Ace Robinson - Lismore Detective and tracker

Hekan Nabbu - African Crime - Australian Federal Police

David Lang - Agent with African Crime division

Jake Carter bouncer at Nimbin Hotel

Others - Horace's Mum Florence, his deceased Dad Harold, Beryl and Mabel Fobsworth, Jim Flood plumber, Gary Sparks electrician, Mr and Mrs Fred Baker, the special pets, Speed, Goof and Fart. Various real estate agents, funeral directors, and senior travellers....

PROLOGUE

Love is a currency spend it wisely

When was the last time you looked at a two headed two-dollar coin? What is it anyhow? A gold trinket, made for limited exchange of small items in a growing number of two-dollar shops. It is mostly worthless in today's inflated world, but if it could talk, what grand stories it could tell. It's all about size and texture and very rarely do you notice the imprinted markings.

Only one in a hundred people would notice a poetic inscription in lieu of a Royal head. Our coin had two sides to it's being. One side had a story so powerful, and so Australian, that it brings into question many of the issues that trouble us today.

The Aboriginal on this coin is Gwoya Jungarai. He was the survivor of an Aboriginal massacre. His people captured his image in art. With his long flowing beard and a powerful chest crossed with tribal scars, he is a man standing proud beneath the

Southern Cross. He is our man on our two-dollar coin. The flip side came out blank, the Queen of England, a distant country, was missing. The inscription on this side, *'love is a currency, spend it wisely'*, would only be found by a few, and the connections within their lives

would relate to the words.

Apart from the written word, the author called (C) has a voice, via the coin as it changes hands. Who better to comment on this epic journey?

This is a story of a trip around Australia, meeting strangers and characters with various and nefarious habits. It is spiced with the sour lemon of death, the sweet honey of humour, and the arid and wet wonders of our vast ocean lapping continent. All this is told through the eyes and words of Horace Winterbottom an English travel writer. Horace involves himself with the characters of Australia. Exchanging the coin becomes a payment. Love is a currency, and it does not always get spent wisely. There is the love of vengeance and unrequited passion. There are life changes, which involve fear, hate, and just plain good and bad luck. The coin carries more than just a message, it offers hope.

From lustful flings, great white shark encounters, exotic animal theft, the illegal diamond trade, Broome sunsets, Aboriginal characters, and top-end Darwinian encounters, the tale evolves. It flows with blunt humour, loose tongues, and sharp knives. It is a tale bookended with swords of lust, want, hate, and desire. There are numerous characters, all connectable within six degrees of separation. Then there is always the chance of unexpected love, even for Horace.

PRELUDE

Peter Simple's last thoughts

"Oh, how the coin's words, *'Love is a currency spend it wisely'*, haunted me as I faced my own demise. These huge dark men ripped off my backpack, then dragged me across a concrete path. I could feel the pain from gravel rash on my hands. There was blood dripping from my nose, and I remember that coin falling out of my shirt pocket, they were my last thoughts."

'(C... oh no not again)'.

An interview with Horace

Horace was dressed like a Cotswold funeral director. He had a classic Derby Bowler hat on his lap, he sat opposite an agent, who introduced himself as Hekan Nabbu, a tall Sudanese Australian, from the African Crime division of the Australian Federal Police. Horace saw the funny side to the man's trade name, but he went on to explain what he had witnessed at the café:

"I heard a car pull up near the adjacent alley. Then men shouting. I left my table in the café and poked my head out the door. I saw that Pimple lad, being set upon by those two African thugs. They were the same African men I saw at Anna Bay. The thugs punched the lad to the ground, screaming 'give us that'! They grabbed at his backpack and ripped it off him. The victims head bounced on the gutter and then he went silent, he may have been unconscious. They then dragged him into the alley, the brutes had one leg each. A minute later your Federal agent Dave Lang pulled up and ran into the alley, with a pistol in his hand. That's when I went back in the café and rang the police. A few minutes later I heard two shots, then I saw one of the thugs run out of the alley holding the backpack and drive off, it was a Toyota Landcruiser, I think. I gingerly went out to the scene; guns always scare me. As I approached the alley entrance the other thug came running out, holding his head. I speculate here, but he may have been wounded. Then the lad Dave came running out chasing the thug. I called out to him that I had rang the Police. I looked in the alley and that lad Pimple was there with a Bowie knife in his chest. He was deceased. It was just ten minutes later when the police arrived. I thought they were very prompt.

There was one other coincidence, just after the Africans had dragged that Pimple lad into the alley, a man who I recognised as Marcus Canning, you may know the lad as 'the Bobbitt of Lavender Bay', walked past. It was just before your agent Dave arrived. Marcus had a dazed look on his face like his mind was elsewhere. He didn't peer into the alley and didn't seem to notice anything unusual. I noticed him pick up something tiny from the path. I believe it was a coin. The strangest thing was, he was carrying a Samurai sword."

CHAPTER 1... APRICOT AND SOCKS

L ife for a peculiar two-dollar coin, like all others, gestated in the Australian Mint. It was bought to the world in a brown paper wrapper and was born into the cash register of Marcus Canning.

(C...call this my birthday)

As Marcus snapped open the pack of coins the first coin to fall out was blank on one side. He thought it was rather strange as the rest were all regular currency. He took the coin to be an omen of some kind and decided to keep it as a talking point. Later that day he took it to Jacks key cutting business next door and had it engraved.

(C...it didn't hurt)

He thought of a few nice poetic pieces but settled on, *'Love is a currency spend it wisely'*. It would make a great gift for Sally with a gold chain on it. Marcus slipped it into his pocket and went back to making coffees.

Cafés like the one that Marcus ran were nearly as common as coins. As an astute young marketing graduate, he knew he needed an attractive name and a good gimmick to kick start the trade and bring in the customers. The name was the easy part, he had thought that one up in High School, *'The Tree House Café'*. The gimmick followed from that. The whole shop was done up like a kid's tree house. Logs, rope ladders, rusty tools and pans and a selection of old books gave it the decor. Antiques and brick-and-brac were also offered for sale to add to the shop's income. As a kid growing up, he and his sister built many a tree house in the ancient oak tree that virtually filled their backyard. His father Harry was a chippy, a carpenter who always had materials like timber and nails at hand, and Band-Aids for the crushed thumbs. Marcus and his sister Susan were a pigeon pair to Harry and Ruth. The carpentry trade had its ups and downs. They moved to Parramatta during one recession when Susan was going through the teenage tantrum stage. Marcus was doing well at school and was heading for a Marketing career. Susan hated school and was into animals, she had many pets. When she was eighteen, she was working part time at the Castle Hill Koala Park, but she never settled. She had a huge fight with Harry and Ruth and left home. They tried many ways to contact her but, in the end, had to list her as a missing person. Finally, after three months she left a message on the phone, she had moved to Western Australia. After that they received an occasional birthday and Christmas card. The family thought they would never see her again.

Marcus was more successful, he was onto something with the business, because crowds came. Childhood memories apparently held sway over the trendy coffee set of Lavender Bay. Above the shop was a comfortable two-bedroom unit, which Marcus, and his childhood sweetheart Sally, called home. One bedroom was their love nest. Decorated by Sally in a sweet but childish 'Barby meets Ken in Copacabana' fashion. The other room was Marcus's man cave or dog kennel, subject to Sally's mood. He was into historic weaponry and heraldry, so his room looked more like a museum from a Scottish castle.

Fiona Sharpe virtually fell into Marcus Canning's

life via a stumble with a hot coffee, just seconds before Marcus received the coffee back, without the cup. The event led to instant stimulation. For one it was love at first sight, for the other it was first degree burns and pain in more ways than just coffee scalds. As Marcus-in-pain apologised and reached for his handkerchief to mop up the spill, the two-dollar coin fell on the floor and the ever-efficient shop assistant Anne, put it in the till. So, our two-dollar coin inadvertently made-up part of Fiona's change.

(C...time to move on)

She was an attractive lady with the sort of figure that attracted wandering eyes. Sally the ever-faithful girlfriend of Marcus would not have been impressed with his thoughts at that moment. That afternoon Fiona placed the two-dollar coin that Marcus had given her in a Waterford crystal tray on her bedside table. She was observant enough to read the coin's inscription and had taken it as an offer from Marcus. It now represented a trinket of her desire and ill perceived future.

(C...shameless Jezebel)

Over the next week Fiona popped in for coffee daily. Her insatiable appetite for perfect love now had a focal point and unknown to Marcus he was her meal. He on the other hand saw her as a sexy plaything, that his ego could not resist. Sally worked at the local chemist in North Sydney, but her real skill was shown when she picked up her banjo. Every weekend she would demonstrate that skill, busking for some extra tax-free money down at the Circular Quay waterfront, for the crowds who couldn't afford Opera House tickets.

For Marcus, who always had Saturday's off, this offered a great chance to consummate his now raging desire for Fiona. He met Fiona at Clark Park, and they walked hand in hand to her one-bedroom flat in Milson Point. It was the home of a minimalist, squeaky clean tiled floor and just enough furniture to make it work. She exited her bathroom stark naked with an apricot-coloured rose between her teeth, she smiled to see Marcus sitting on the edge of the bed, like a schoolboy in trouble with the principle. He was in his white bonds with black socks still on, but his manhood was erect like a snow-covered Everest. He looked at her with lust, she was gorgeous and shimmered all over with a heavy coating of apricot body dew. Let the fun begin she yelled and jumped on Marcus with a tidal wave of passion. In a slight dampening of their magic moment, she slipped off him and onto the floor. On the second attempt she was more successful.

They had three sessions that morning, first took minutes the last an hour of love, lust, and pleasure. Marcus was on a high, he laid with her for an hour smothered by the captivating smells of sex and apricots. She laughed a lot and then her demeanour fluctuated between looks of wanting and smiles of delight. Marcus, who was still on a curve of awe, was unaware that her capricious smile was a precursor to the way she could react to rejection, hate, fear, and pain. The movie *'Play misty for me'*, had found a sequel, but Marcus who was now in heaven had never seen it. The terms of endearment flowed, he even had a nickname for her, he called her his little apricot and she responded in kind and called him socks. On Saturdays for the next three months Apricot and Socks were the *'Bonny and Clyde lovers'* of Milson Point.

It was on a windy September morning that Marcus

decided his lustful relationship must end. It wasn't just the feeling Sally was starting to get suspicious about what he did on Saturdays, it was more the fact that Fiona was exercising more demands on the direction of their union. Marcus would be upfront and straight to the point. He was totally unprepared for her reaction. On the day before, Fiona had been to a garage sale and had bought Marcus a token of her love for him. She knew he collected swords from history and the WW2 Samurai sword was a bargain.

She expected Marcus to arrive early and had prepared a champaign breakfast. A romantic start to a day of lust. She had purchased two bottles of her favourite bubbles, a fruit platter, bacon and eggs and an assortment of pastries. By the time Marcus arrived one bottle had been consumed and she was hot to trot for session one. Marcus held back on his news until session one, breakfast and the last bottle of bubbles had been enjoyed. They sat there in their nakedness glowing from the feast. He was feeling free of inhibitions and totally tactless, as most men are when they have had their treats.

(C...for those who feel faint at the sight of blood, best skip the next two paragraphs)

Fiona was inebriated when the words finally flowed:

"Fiona, I want today's encounter to be our last, I feel it's past its use by date and it's time we both moved on."

Shock is probably not a powerful enough word, Fiona shrilled with anger, then just as quick she smiled and tried to get him back to bed with a coy expression. When this failed, she toyed and laughed:

"Oh! you're just joking, you can't be serious, what about this!"

She had picked up the sword and removed it slowly from the scabbard:

"I'll slice your man hood off; you won't be sharing that with anyone!"

"Don't be silly Fiona, I mean it's over, let's just part as friends."

What happen next is open to conjecture, in the court hearing she said it was an accident caused by too much alcohol. In Marcus's recollection she threatened him prior to the slashing before he passed out. What actually happened, was that due in part to Marcus's shock. He staggered, slipped on his own blood, and knocked himself out on the bedside table. Due to her quick response to the emergency, she was shown some leniency, but the jury still found her guilty of malicious wounding.

(C...she wasn't a complete Jezebel)

The sword was razor sharp, accident or not, it chopped of the tip of Marcus's Everest in a split second. His jaw dropped, blood spurted, and Fiona screamed just as he passed out.

Escape was Fiona's only muddled thought, she composed herself and held in her panic. She stopped the bleeding by an elastic band on his stump, placed the severed part in a plastic bag and put it in the fridge. She then rang for an Ambulance and packed a bag with some of her most valuable possessions. She checked Marcus was still breathing and placed a pillow under his head to make him a little more comfortable. She then left a note on the door that his part was in the freezer. On the way out she picked up the shiny coin from her bedside table, (C...lucky me), and fled in a disillusioned panic, leaving the door ajar. The *'Apricot and Socks'* tags faded out and were now mixed memories in the currency of love.

The thoughtful fridge placement and fast paramedics were the only legacies that Marcus could take with him on that windy Saturday. He came around in the Ambulance to the sounds of a siren and someone saying *'Bobbitt'* on the radio, The announcer continued:

'John Wayne Bobbitt from Virginia USA was the man who had his penis cut off with a kitchen knife as he slept, by his wife Lorena in 1993'.

With that, Marcus passed out again.

Tears welled in Fiona's now red eyes, as she wandered across the Harbor Bridge, not sure what to do. She made her way down the stairs at the Rocks towards the ferry terminal. Her sadness plateaued for a moment when she heard the soft strumming of a banjo. The lady was playing a tune that Fiona's mother used to sing when she was a child. She sat there for a few moments watching Sally's skill mesmerise the audience. As she headed off into an unknown future in a daze, she deposited her shiny new two-dollar coin of unrequited love into Sally's cap, smiled and said thanks.

(C...at least I didn't roll into the Harbour that would have been a quick end to this tale)

From the ferry to Manly, she had made her way north by bus to Palm Beach, without attracting any attention. She then caught the lunchtime ferry to Patonga. While disembarking the ferry, she slipped on a wet step. Her anguish and guilt finally hit home, the tears flowed again, and she broke down. This attracted the attention of a friendly by-standing tourist named Horace Winterbottom.

Horace consoled Fiona for a minute, and then offered her to share an Uber to the railway station at Woy-Woy, and perhaps a drink at the Bay View Hotel.

(C... at this stage I'm not sure if Horace is a protagonist or an antagonist)

His empathy was short lived, the true damage of what she had inflicted on Marcus came to the fore. Fiona spilled out the tale of horror with flooding tears. In true British form, Horace offered her a brandy at the hotel to calm the situation. While away at the bar he contacted the Police with the grizzly story. He then purchased the brandy and a beer for himself. He returned to find a more subdued Fiona now playing the poker machines and being chatted up by a gruesome looking bloke called Scrags. Horace knew this because someone yelled out:

"Scrags it's your shout."

As a gentleman the frugal Pommy managed to get Fiona's attention without causing any drama with the local bar fly. He offered her the brandy, and asked for its six dollars cost, he did pay for his own beer. Minutes later the Police arrived, and a sad and sorry Fiona was escorted off to a life in love's shadow and hate's nightmares. Despite the shock, Horace was quite taken with her honesty and sweet disposition and followed them out to the Paddy wagon. Scrags, real name Scotty Banister, had no sweet disposition and gave Horace a dirty look as he left the bar. To this low life an easy prospect had just gone begging.

Sally was a forgiving soul. While Marcus was on the mend in hospital, after the luck of locating and reattaching his manhood, Sally ran the coffee shop. She took some holiday time off from the Chemist but maintained her busking. On some Saturdays she could make as much as two hundred dollars in coins, not always gold ones. This additional tax-free income was never banked. Instead, Sally got into the habit of saving the gold coins in a various array of piggybanks on the shelves. These became talking points and enhanced the atmosphere of the Tree House Cafe. The special gold coin went unseen by Sally, and it was now having a vacation of its own, inside the belly of a ceramic piggy bank that took the form of a rather cute Koala bear.

(C... that is better than being pork barrelled)

While Marcus was still mending in Hospital, Sally sold the cute Koala to an inquisitive British tourist, named Horace Winterbottom. She emptied all the coins except one, for good luck. By chance the two-dollar coin left in the koala bank, was the one deposited by Fiona. *(C... that's, me)* Horace placed it into his special travel case. It was his vintage school case from his days at the Cotswold School, he used it for all his memorabilia on trips.

Horace had followed Fiona's story through the press, and the three-year prison sentence she received for her act of senseless passion, seemed well judged. He had time on his side, he was on a two-year working visa. So, while in Sydney he decided to visit the Treehouse Café on Lavender Bay Road. The story of Fiona and Marcus had been covered by all the media and the Café was doing a booming trade. People were fascinated by the incident, and although Marcus was not impressed with being called '*The Bobbitt of Lavender Bay*', business was doing great. While at the Café, Horace kept his involvement in the incident to himself, he just wanted to meet the players. When he walked in and said hello to Sally, he noticed a large picture of Marcus from an unknown admirer on the counter. Written in Texta across the bottom where the words, *'Hang in there Bobbitt'*. The background music was softly playing, it was Roy Orbison's rendition of *'Love Hurts'*. Horace drank the last of his coffee and once again thanked Sally for the piggybank. As he left the cafe, he looked her in the eyes and quoted Will Shakespeare:

'If music be the food of love play on'.

Marcus recuperated at his mother's place for a month before Sally would accept him back. He arrived home with grateful contrition and a few weeks later their love making was evaluated and found to be in full working order. He and Sally were now engaged and moving on in the currency of love.

✻ ✻ ✻

The travel diary Horace was writing needed good yarns. He was a soft-hearted soul and would soon start sending Fiona, who was now a resident at Silverwater Prison, an occasional postcard from his various ports of call. His around Australian odyssey was about to commence. He had visited all the major cities and the southeast corner of the country in the past. On this adventure he intended to follow the well-worn tourist track in a clockwise direction, and occasionally do a *'Dirk Gently,'* to follow a storyline.

Horace was also a collector of trinkets, and he had with him his vintage school case from his days at Cotswold Grammar, and in it he would place special memories of his travels.

CHAPTER 2... NULLARBOR DIVERSION

Horace was on Central Station searching for someone to guide him to the Indian Pacific train. All the signage was like hieroglyphics to him. He had been all over the world, but multicultural Sydney, with the plethora of different accents made understanding directions a challenge. Finally, an Indian Australian gentleman guided him to the departure point. The sleeping compartment on the train was little more than a shoe box. From his tiny window the starting vista was of red rooves and graffiti, eventually trees started to appear.

When the train crossed the Nepean River at Penrith, the Blue Mountains of forests and craggy gullies, were an inspiring escape into the wild. They weren't even blue, they were green. He read on a brochure that they only appeared blue from the distance, because of the eucalyptus haze. As time went on, the trees thinned out into grasslands and orange plains. To Horace the constant blue sky and flat orange earth became boring. It was only broken by the occasional spinifex scrub, scraggy trees, and rocky hills. Occasionally, he would see, a kangaroo, a dingo and even a camel. The strange thing was, that before Broken Hill, it was mostly roadkill and goats. He thought that collecting goats in the outback could be a lucrative trade.

The dining car and bar offered the best treats. Horace's ideas about Australian names were reinforced.

It was a retirees express. He met Jim Flood, a former plumber, and Gary Sparks, a former electrician. Both were travelling with their wives. One other chap named Walter was travelling by himself, his wife had recently died from breast cancer. They had always planned to do this trip but left it too late. Horace got on well with Walter, they ate together in the dining car, and both enjoyed a beer afterwards. Walter told Horace to call him Wal, but not Wally. He had copped more than his fair share of 'Where's Wally' humour in his life. Wal was a doctor and still working as a Proctologist. Afterwards he gave a full run down on colonoscopies, and the need to have one, to avoid bowel cancer. Horace then tried to change the subject to his beloved William Shakespeare.

"Walter, did you know that the moons around Uranus are named after Shakespeare's Oberon, Arial, and Juliet?"

"No, I didn't, in my profession we call them haemorrhoids. At university Horace, they called me the proctologist bard, because of my love of Shakespeare and my initials being W S. Fart jokes were all the rage back then. One of my favourites was love is like elevator flatulence; it brings both smiles and gasps."

This had Horace in stitches of laughter, he was enjoying this man's company. Thankfully they both had other interests, and most of their following conversations were about travel destinations. Horace avoided the bacon and eggs the following morning, and just had 'Bran Flakes' and fruit. He did have a chuckle to himself when he found out Walter's last name was Shakeshaft. They spent the next few days talking and touring together. Walter was a bit like one of Horace's childhood mates from school, Hugo Firth. Hugo was always the polite one, and a true gentleman. He was born with a lisp and the school kids gave him a tough time about his chivalrous name.

The stop over at Broken Hill was a treat. The Palace Hotel was the first port of call. They were told about the wonderful landscape murals on the walls, and a copy of Botticelli's Venus on the ceiling. Horace even bought a small print of the painting for the collectable memories in his vintage school case. The original hotel was erected in the late nineteenth century as a coffee palace for the Temperance Movement, a group of coffee and tea drinking ladies. The coffee palace was unprofitable, and ultimately became a licensed hotel. At that time there were more than seventy pubs in and around town. Wal and Horace had the choice of only twenty now.

The Adelaide stop was a non-event, just a quick pick up of some more travellers. It wasn't on Horace's visit list; he had spent a week there five years prior. His notes read:

"The fun place was Glenelg. In the city, visiting a church, museum, or watching traffic lights change, were the best options."

It was here that another couple joined them in the dining car, they were, Mr and Mrs Fred Baker, who had a 'Bakers Delight' franchise.

The Indian Pacific arrived in Kalgoorlie right on time. Horace and Walter had one last beer at the Station Inn, and they exchanged details.

Horace sculled the last of his beer, quoting, 'bottoms up old lad.'

"In my profession Horace we prefer analogies over euphemisms."

"All's well that ends well Wal."

They parted ways with a handshake and having a good laugh.

Kalgoorlie was warmer than Horace expected, but it was a pleasant warmth. He had allowed two days in this town of gold but didn't expect to get rich. The mining companies controlled the place. Horace's only prospecting will be in the train ride to Perth, it was called 'The Prospector'. He walked past the Post Office and sent postcards to Fiona in Silverwater prison, and others to his Mum Florence, and Beryl, his over friendly neighbour back in the Cotswolds. Afterwards he found just the right spot at 'Paddy's Ale House,' for a room and another cold beer. His room was air conditioned and overlooked the main street. Horace dropped his bags off and headed to the bar. He was in a chatty mood, as was Nancy Coogan, the voluptuous publican. They were exchanging travel stories when Horace noticed a boomerang on the shelf above the bar. It was a work of art and appeared to be handmade. "Does it come back?" asked Horace.

"Not if you take it," she responded with a smirk of country humour.

It had a Dream-time serpent painted on it, and Horace wanted it for his travel collections.

"Can I buy that off you Nancy?", asked Horace.

She responded bluntly, "no, it's not for sale! These are traveller gifts, and I will only exchange with trinkets that have a better story attached."

Horace pondered his options, smiled, and offered up the 'Bobbitt of Lavender Bay' story. He then went to his room for his vintage school case and pulled out the Koala piggy bank. The deal was done, Nancy felt like the winner, she rattled it and said:

"It's even got a coin!" *('C...that woke me up')* "The boomerang was left by a local Aboriginal they called *'Walkabout Jimmy'*, as a payment in kind for the damaged caused in a punch up a month earlier. I was glad to be rid of anything to do with Jimmy, he was a pain."

Our travel writer had another story, so both thought they got a good deal.

"One more thing Nancy, how does it work?"

She grabbed it back and gave a demonstration.

"You're right-handed? Ok, hold it with the rounded side facing your body, like this, and the boomerang pointing in the direction you intend to throw it. If there is a breeze in your face throw it to the right of the wind, and watch it come back. It's that easy."

"Thanks Nancy, I'll give it a go this afternoon, if you hear an Ambulance, you'll know it didn't work." He laughed, and Nancy sniggered and wished him good luck.

It all went spectacularly well; Horace found a park close to the hotel and launched the boomerang as per the instructions. It went as predicted, an aeronautical marvel of Aboriginal design. As it turned in the air Horace imagined it missing its intended prey and returning to his feet. That last part didn't go to plan. The killing native missile was approaching his head at and extreme speed. He had an image of decapitation, and in the last moments ducked for cover. The boomerang landed just a metre from him. He was a bit shaken but truly impressed with his newfound skill. The returning marvel would now be placed in his antique school case, become another memory in his journey, and most likely never used again.

A week after Horace acquired the boomerang, *'Walkabout Jimmy'* went directly from Centrelink to the pub to bargain for its return. In its normal place on the shelf was a smiling koala piggy bank. Jimmy was peeved, he loved that boomerang and was going to buy it back. The bar was empty, so Jim snatched the koala bank, and did a runner, only later to find it contained a miserable two bucks for his trouble.

(C...I felt insulted, just a miserable two bucks)

Jimmy, with a thumb out, was trudging along his song-line back to his country. Esperance was where he belonged; he was a Pujari man. His days in Kalgoorlie and Boulder were not all pleasant memories, because at times racism had an evil undercurrent. He had lost a good mate in a suspicious car impact and was wary at night, especially after a few beers in the park. With luck, Aunty Gwen was heading south and picked him up in the family Ute. The first thing he did was to show her his koala piggy bank.

Jim rattled the piggy bank, and said:

"Not much of a saver, am I Aunty?"

He laughed and extracted the coin, then became aware it was inscribed:

"Check this out, it's got a story on it, *'love is a currency spend it wisely'*, crikey", said Jimmy:

"If that was you and I Aunty we would be love millionaires".

Jim got dropped off at the Pier Hotel in Esperance, packed the Koala in his swag, thanked Aunty Gwen and went off to find his fishing mate Bill.

'Likeable Billy' was easy to find, same spot in the beer garden he was in two years ago. Back then the pub was getting a bit yuppified and a bit unfriendly to locals, but

now it seemed things had settled back a bit.

Billy's big grin was a welcome sign:

"G'day Cuz, what's the plan then?"

"Just a couple of beers here mate, we don't want to wear out our welcome. Then we get a slab of VB from Woollies, and then back to the camp for a family catch up. Tomorrow, we get some bait from Joes and catch us a couple of two kilo bream at Bandy Creek. What do you say to that mate?"

"It's just what I was thinking Cuz."

Happiness is meant to be shared, this was Jim's first thought when he got to the camp and met up with the clan. Everyone had a smile on their face, there was little material wealth here, but there was a mountain of love and wellbeing. Some of the family made a bit of income out at the Pink Lake salt works, but the majority lived day by day on Government money. It didn't really matter, they were family in country and as Aunt Gwen would say: "I am the land, I don't have to own it."

With his *'Walkabout Jimmy'* grin, he told of his adventures in Boulder, and about trading up his boomerang for a koala piggy bank, all the camp kids listened and laughed. Jim was one for making theatre out of simple things. His exaggeration and embellished tales continued all night until tied eyes and beer swagger had the clan drifting off. Jim spent the night outdoors on his swag. It was a clear cool spring night, and the Milky Way was in full splendour.

(C...we should all be so lucky)

Just prior to sleep he placed the coin back in the koala, mainly for luck. He was thinking about its inscription and how rich he was with family love. It was good to be home.

The next day Bill and Jim packed their gear and headed off for a couple of days fishing at Bandy Creek. Bill's well-worn and rusty Hyundai was only reliable enough for short trips around town, but it would get them to the fishing and back. There was nothing better than fresh fish cooked over an open fire and washed down with a cold beer, so, they stopped off at Esperance for supplies.

A local biker group known as 'The Great Aussie Blight,' were parked at the shops when the Hyundai pulled up. Bill was still a little worse for wear from the previous night's session and accidentally nudged the closest bike. The bike's owner was Ajax Rider, an ill-tempered southwest Sydney boy, who had attitude to burn. He was the youngest member of this bike tribe; most were greying retirees. Their leader, a saddle-hardened road warrior they called Mozzy, let him join thinking he could settle Ajax's anger management issues, it was a challenging task. No-one was aware that Mozzy was a teacher in his younger days, his real name was Morrice H Davidson, and of course the H was for Harley. Ajax was initiated into the tribe, given his 'Grim Reaper' tattoo, and he seemed to be adjusting. He had moved to Esperance to get away from some drug deal indiscretions, and police warrants, when he met Mozzy at the Pier Hotel. He looked like a typical Sydney bikie, shaved head, three-day growth, and a gold chain necktie, but Ajax's had a small leather pouch on the chain, in which he kept life memories. Hearing the stories in that pouch was the reason Mozzy asked him to join the group.

Ajax was about a hundred metres away when he saw his bike being inspected by a couple of local Koori's, as he called them. To say Ajax was racist was an understatement. He picked up an empty long-neck bottle and ran towards the Hyundai. Bill saw the fury on Ajax's face and made for the driver's seat:

"Let's get out of here Jimmy, this guy looks like he's losing it."

Jim was at the passenger's door but was less concerned. He raised his hands over his head and yelled:

"Whoa! there mate, no damage done, it was just a nudge."

This had no sway at all with the approaching thug. Jim dodged the first blow, which smashed into the Hyundai. What was left of the bottle became a jagged glass weapon. It was obvious to Jim that this bloke would now make him bleed a little. In the moment that he had to avoid Ajax's next move, Jim reached into his swag, sadly the koala piggy bank was his only available weapon. He smashed it against Ajax's head. The biker went down on his knees in stunned silence, Jim grabbed the opportunity to escape, screaming:

"Time to bolt Billy! "

Bill was laughing with nervous excitement as he sped off:

"Did you see the look on that bozo's face mate? A pig brought down by a piggy bank."

Jimmy was of two minds; he was glad to get away unscathed, but he couldn't help thinking about the bikers' aggressive attitude. He thought he had seen enough of that hatred in Boulder. It was then he realised, that his inscribed coin went with the koala piggy bank. He smiled when he thought that in this case the currency of aggression was spent unwisely. He turned to Billy, with a hidden sadness, and a questioning thought about life choices: Billy was still on a high, when Jimmy changed the subject:

"Come on mate, forget that idiot, we'll get the bait at Bandy Creek and then catch some real whoppers."

Ajax was on the side of the road bleeding slightly from his ear when their tribe leader Mozzy came over to see why he was playing in the gutter. No one in his group had seen the incident, so he decided to keep silent about it, to save face.

"What's with the broken koala Jaxxy?" Asked Mozzy.

"Ah! some wanker in a passing car just threw it at me." Ajax responded in temper.

As he looked at the broken pieces of ceramics, he picked up the two-dollar coin and read the inscription, *'Love is a currency spend it wisely.'* Deep down in his damaged soul the pun hit a raw nerve.

In a tough retort he said to his mate:

"The car was a rusty Hyundai, driven by two Kooris, they're on borrowed time."

Ajax, still in a rage, sat in the gutter and leant back on his hands, and his right hand squished into a fresh dog deposit. In a strange twist of mood, he just laughed to himself, it all seemed to sum up his current life.

Ajax had a small leather pouch on a gold chain around his neck. Its where he kept some of his life-time trinkets, that's where he placed the coin. (C...*Thankfully with his clean hand*). It now sat next to his old girlfriend Sandy's engagement ring, a past broken heart. Also, in the pouch was a Catholic Cross from his days as an Alter boy, a tormenting memento. In Homer's *'Iliad'*, Ajax was known as the *'Bulwark of the Achaeans'*; described as fearless, strong, and powerful. Ajax of *'The Great Australian Blight'*, may have had some of those qualities, but sadly, after his childhood experiences, he had been damaged goods for most of his life. *'Poseidon the God of War'* wouldn't strike down this Ajax; his existence may have ended on a two wheeled coffin if he wasn't taken down by something else in the ocean of life. It seems he was the one on borrowed time.

(C... *This is the Nullarbor diversion, don't fret, Horace will be back soon*)

CHAPTER 3... A POUCH OF PAIN

Ajax was a tough bloke, but after the incident with that ceramic pig, he was riding on a high of anger and this led to a bit of depression. Amongst his peers, within the Great Australian Blight bike pack, he was often seen as a loner. So, when he said to several of them that he would spend a few days in Esperance, they weren't bothered. He told Mozzy that he would catch up in Albany. They were all staying at the local caravan park, and they took off on their ride the next day. It was in the Pier Hotel that Ajax ran into a guy who was running a shark diving boat off Cull Island. Ethan Burlington was a big man with a laconic grin, what startled Ajax was Ethan's left hand, it was an appliance. It looked like the love child of torsion bars and multigrips. Prosthetics had come a long way since this contraption was put together, but Ethan said it was all he needed. Ajax needed something to grin at and take his mind off his bout of depression. Ethan's hand monstrosity, and shark close ups, fitted the bill. So, he signed up for a diving experience.

Ajax woke the following morning and was feeling a lot better, He was now looking forward to the shark dive. Ethan had been running his cage dive company off Cull Island since 2000 and it had been a very popular business. But on this day Ajax was his only client. He met Ethan at the wharf at 10am that morning, it was a blue-sky day with a slight breeze blowing from the south.

"It's a perfect day for Great Whites and memories mate," said Ethan, as Ajax approached.

"Yes, looking forward to it Ethan, something to brag about in Albany."

"Everybody calls me Burley down here Ajax."

"Ok Burley no sweat, so long as you're the burley and not me! By the way how did you lose your hand?"

"Blind shark choices Ajax, hand and tuna too close together and slow reflexes after a heavy night."

Cull Island was one of hundreds of small islands and rocky outcrops that form the Recherche Archipelago off the Esperance coast. The island had little vegetation on it, and just a few goats who were the sole inhabitants. It was a popular destination for fishing, snorkelling, and diving, because it supported abundant marine life, including the great white shark. There had been eighteen fatal shark attacks in Western Australia since 2000, but most of these facts were unknown to Ajax, he was there for a thrill, not knowledge.

Some companies chum or burley the water to attract sharks. Some tie off large chunks of tuna to a rope off the cage, Ethan Burlington did both, his nickname Burley had two meanings. Burley dealt with the lifting boom, attached the cage, and lowered it into the water. It was a still day, and the blue water of the Great Southern Ocean was inviting and clear. The only cloudy bit was the chumming trail, a mixture of the captains special burley, for which he was famous. This method of shark attractant was slightly illegal and frowned upon by certain people in the local tourist establishments. They thought it bought too much danger to other water-based activities. As far as Burley was concerned, size mattered, and big sharks bought big rewards.

Ajax stood on the bow of the boat in a full wet suit. He was still wearing his gold chain with the leather pouch attached, it was tucked under his chest piece. Burley gave Ajax the final instructions on the operation of the tank, the breathing apparatus, and the safety procedures. Ajax was now on a high, the pending excitement subdued all his troubles, this shark dive was something he had always wanted to do. For a moment his mind went back to the message on that coin, *'love is a currency, at what price',* he thought. To Ajax hate had more value, and the only spending he would do today was this dive. It was a chance to go one on one with a real predator not a robe wearing man of God.

The cage was a solid unit made from stainless steel rods; it had portals of about fourty square centimetres on all four sides. The cage was open at the bottom with diagonal corner braces. This allowed the diver footings and an entry point; it was a fairly safe experience. There was only ever one incident where a great white crashed into a cage, and in this case the shark suffered more damage.

Burley hooked a large piece of tuna on to the cage. Ajax saw the tuna, trembled with a laugh, and asked; *'rather that than me, eh?* He then jumped overboard as instructed, and quickly swam to the cage. It was an exhilarating moment when he thought he was at his most vulnerable. Two small reef sharks swam by, as did a school of reasonably sized fish, that Ajax thought were bream. He had only ever caught two fish in his life, a bream and a flathead at Nelson Bay. He was half-drunk after a hard night of booze, birds, and bashings, at the Seaview Pub. He remembered those days well. It was at the Bay he received his first tattoo, a skunk on his left arm. Those days of riding adventures with his old group the Skunks, were just memories now. The *'Grim Reaper'* with a sickle, on his right arm, came later. All members of the *'Great Aussie Blight'* had it. It was an initiate's rite of passage.

Ajax looked through the portal in the direction of the burley trail, the reef sharks and the fish suddenly disappeared, and all was still. There was a grey black blur in his peripheral vision, it moved at a frightening speed. Through his goggles, in the distance, he saw the blur turn in all its majesty, it was a five to six metre monster white, and it now swam directly at the cage. Ajax had an adrenaline rush and a brief thought to make a dash for the boat. He stood his ground and his blood pressure hit a high note. The shark lunged at the bait and accidentally hit the side of the cage. When a great white shark lunges and bites something, it is temporarily blinded. They also cannot swim backwards. So, with a bit of luck it did not get its massive head stuck in the portal. Instead, it just wrestled with the large piece of tuna, oblivious to the fact that the observer was no longer interested.

Ajax at 36, was not one for doctors, and despite little exercise, smoking, and a heavy meat diet, he always thought that he was fairly fit. He had no concept of the term, coronary artery calcium scoring. For if he did, he may have taken measures to find out what the score of one thousand meant. In his case it was ninety percent blockages in his widow maker heart arteries. At the high note of the great white shark advance, his heart and all the loveless hurt that it contained failed him. In death's final few seconds he clutched at his chest and leather pouch and had a fleeting thought of dog poo. Ajax drifted out the bottom of the cage and the current took him off to visit *'Poseidon the God of the Sea'*.

(C...don't panic, I will be rescued)

Burley was at a loss to know what happened. He saw the shark strike the bait and thought that Ajax had got his money's worth. When he raised the cage and found his client was missing shock and insurance fears prevailed. After he made the calls for help, distress over the tragedy set in. A coastal sea search persisted for three days before they gave up. No blood in the water at the initial site and a strong current was enough for the coroner to rule death by miss-adventure, a possible medical incident. There was no memorial service for Ajax. His extended warrants in Sydney indicated that he had no family. The *Great Australian Blight* bike group were notified by Police in Albany, but none of the group were interested in going back to Esperance at that time. Mozzy told the Police about Ajax's ex-girlfriend Sandy in Lakemba and her address. It took a while, but eventually Sandy received a cheque in the mail from the sale of Ajax bike. One would hope she spent it wisely.

CHAPTER 4... A CROSS, A RING, A COIN

Horace, our travel writer for *'Finding Earth Magazine'*, had just arrived at East Perth station on the Indian Pacific rail. It was a fantastic trip, and the Nullarbor leg allowed a great deal of catch-up writing time. He was now hanging out for a good strong cup of tea and a sandwich. The Whistle Stop Café at the station provided the perfect spot. It was here he notice the front-page article on the West Australian newspaper. It was about Great White sharks dying on drum lines off Margaret River's Gracetown beach.

'Sharks', he thought, *'what a horrible way to go'.*

The paper went on to say that drum lines, although contentious with some, were the only security from shark attack at Gracetown beach. The other choice was not to surf or swim. Horace picked up his hire car and headed south to Bunbury and the Margaret River. Shark stories had piqued his interest.

Horace had taken his time heading south. This coastline had many attractions. He visited the shipwreck museum in Freemantle. He stayed at an up-market resort on the beach at Mandurah and then stopped at Lake Clifton to look in wonder at the two-thousand-year-old Thrombolite steppingstones. He drove through Bunbury and walked the southern hemisphere's longest timber jetty in Busselton. One of Horace's most exciting experiences was the limestone cave called N-gilgi, at Yallingup. He was astonished to learn that these cave systems ran down the Western Australian southern coastline and that there were hundreds of magic cave formations just below his feet. He finally arrived at Margaret River and spent the night at a local motel in Gracetown.

The next morning Horace was finishing off his bake beans and egg breakfast at Gracie's General store and decided to drive down to Melaleuca Beach for a paddle. When he arrived, he noticed a gathering across the road, as per usual, Horace was dressed like he was going to a funeral. He took off his shoes and socks and left them in the hire car with his tie and coat. He then rolled is cuffs up to the knees and his shirt sleeves to his elbows. Looking now more like 'Mr Bean' on a summer vacation he made his way on to the beach.

Two kilometres off the coast from Gracetown is the 'Cow-Bombie'. It is a world-renowned big wave ocean surf location. The southerly swell here produces some of Australia's largest waves, they can reach ten metres plus. It is not a place for the faint hearted, nor burley trails that attract White Pointers. Sharks are one of the most powerful species of predator in the ocean and without a doubt on this part of the Margaret River coast in Western Australia they were feared the most. The Department of Primary Industry had responsibility for deployment of drum lines. When an early morning call was received that a large white pointer had washed up on Gracetown beach, their first call was to Hannah Fisher. Hannah was the go-to girl on this part of the coast. She was a marine biologist with extensive knowledge of the region's sharks. She parked her car at Melaleuca Beach, grabbed her gear and headed across the road to the beach. A lady and a boy were gathered around this large shark carcass. Seagulls were screeching and an alarm siren was going off in the distance.

As Horace walked onto the sand he stopped and spoke to an old lady with a snarl on her face. He introduced himself as Horace Winterbottom of the *'Finding Earth magazine.'*

"Gladys Trussell," she said, thinking she might get into a magazine:

"That's Trussell, with 'SS's not ZZs!"

Horace smiled, "and what do you think has happened here Gladys?"

For subconscious reasons Gladys was not comfortable around men dressed like hobo funeral directors.

"Can't you see, it's a dead shark washed up on the beach, those bloody drumlines kill them!"

Horace sensed her annoyance, thanked her, and approached the dead beast, he noticed that the young boy standing beside his probable mother, was licking an ice cream cone with hundreds and thousands on the top. Horace had a thought:

"I should have bought one of those, it looks delicious."

He quickly changed his thinking when he noticed that the boy licked his ice cream in tune with a green snot-slug sliding in and out of his left nostril. The mother didn't seem too concerned about the nasal care of her child and no handkerchief was forthcoming.

Horace noticed that the shark had a large hole and rip near its mouth.

"Is that what killed it?"

He asked, as he turned his attention to the lady kneeling next to the carcass. The lady had a name tag on, she was Hannah Fisher from the marine biology unit at the University of Western Australia. Horace smiled about her name, and the dead fish she was about to examine. He knelt next to her, she looked at him strangely, and said:

"Most likely bled out after a mammoth struggle to free itself from the hook. If your here to help you can pass me that bag."

He did what she asked, and enquired:

"What type of shark was it?"

Her response was crafted with question annoyance:

"It's a great white, they frequent this area, and if you don't sit back a little you may get covered in its offal."

Hannah removed a large scalpel from the bag and began to slice the shark's stomach. Horace watched in fascination, as did the mother. The boy's eyes and mouth were wide open in anticipation, as ice cream ran down his right hand and dripped on to the shark's head, the green slug had gone back into hiding.

Hannah began to slice and commented that the shark had had a recent kill. Horace gagged at the stench and was astounded to see the amount of smelly material that came flowing out from the shark's belly. As the offal flowed a white appendage slipped out of the shark's gullet. It was an arm, a tattoo indicated that the 'Grim Reaper' had collected it. The mangled hand at the end of the arm was clenched around a piece of neoprene. The stench and horror were now overwhelming, the audience moved back and just stared in disbelief, as what was left of the boy's ice cream dropped into the sand.

Harold stood and brushed the sand off. "What happens now?"

"I notify police, organise a tractor, find a secluded part of the beach and have it buried...deep! Then I write up a report and have a vent to my bosses about bloody drumlines, again!"

As a memento, she cut out two of the shark's largest teeth, gave one to ice cream boy and one to Horace, they both thanked her. Another trinket for Horace's collectable memories in his vintage school case.

The audience sensed that they had worn out their welcome and slowly left the scene. Horace was heading further south, and now had another interesting encounter about sharks and drumlines to write-up. The mother and boy went off to find a tap and a handkerchief. Hannah wrapped the arm for delivery to the police and coroner. Then packed her gear and went to wash up prior to making all the appropriate phone calls. When the offal spewed out, a little leather pouch with a degraded gold chain washed into the sand, none of the party noticed. When he gagged and moved back from the stench, Harold's right knee crushed it deeper beneath the sand.

The Police made the connection with the Esperance tragedy, after asking Mozzy of the 'Great Australian Blight', bike pack about the 'Grim Reaper' tattoo. They notified Sandy for some closure, but she had lost interest in Ajax by then, and was about to be married to an ex-priest.

CHAPTER 5... QUOKKA SEASON

Mrs Gladys Trussell had lived in Gracetown for the past five years since her retirement. She was a fit and spritely lady who walked and swam daily. Her only two vices were, a tipple of brandy at night and no tolerance for fools or strangers. Her son Trevor, who lived in Freemantle, was due for a visit and she was feeling excited.

* * *

The South American drug cartels were a long way from Rottnest Island, off the West Australian coast, but the taint of a different criminal activity had a strong foothold here. Hu Chin was the Australian animals' front man for the lucrative trade in exotic animal exports. The current value crop was Rottnest Island Quokkas. The nocturnal Quokka is a very sociable and friendly animal. On Rottnest Island they are tourist friendly, and easy to catch.

To Hu Chin, October is Quokka season. The joeys are weened and ripe for collection. Quokka meat, like wallaby and kangaroo, is high in protein, low in fat and tasty to some. Being endangered they are extremely rare, and the fines are substantial. Like most exotics, someone is always prepared to pay a premium to criminals. People in Asian markets were taken in by these cute and funny critters. To some they were a tasty delicacy, to others, they loved their fur, and a few were just avid animal pet collectors.

An Indonesian syndicate ran by an unscrupulous criminal named Rizky Lestari, was the boss in this business. His first name meant sustenance and wealth; his life matched his name. Rizky had political connections that turned a blind eye to the trade. He provided the boats and the coordination in many ports around the world, to ensure a smooth transition of product. The Australian end products included snakes, skinks, endangered parrots, and even Australia's beloved Bilby and Quokkas. Hu Chin was his man down under, and he was ruthless. How animal lover Trevor Trussell got mixed up in this industry is a long story which involved money loans and gullibility. Chin had befriended Trevor at a local Freemantle animal protection club and made the offer to support the Trussells animal shelter project.

The debt was acquired from a Chinese businessman in Perth. This man was an associate of Hu Chin and no friend to the Trussell family. The loan for three hundred thousand dollars to Trevor and his wife Susan was unsecured and short on detail, with Mr Hu Chin as guarantor. They didn't realise at the time that their lives were the security for the debt. The funds set up a private animal shelter on a cheap country half acre block near Oldbury about fourty minutes south of Port Freemantle. It was surrounded by farms and forest and had established sheds and a small one-bedroom residence. Fauna victims of local road trauma was the Trussells original motive. The couple were minimalists and although the business would barely keep them off government support, they were in it for the love of animals. Trevor would soon realise that the whole operation was just a front for Hu Chin's export racket. Chin was aware of Trevor's collection skills and knowledge of Australian wildlife, and that his wife Susan was a veterinarian's assistant, with some skills. It was a two-year plan to have leverage over the couple.

After about eighteen months the business was running well. Chin started to apply the pressure for debt repayment. This was the stand-over moment when Chin's true purpose came to the fore. Trevor was informed that he was now going to provide a certain number of Australian species. If he didn't comply, he and his wife might meet with an unfortunate outcome. Trevor was scared and he didn't inform Susan. He now knew the truth of the business assistance; he decided to co-operate. Despite the fear for his wife, the icing on the cake was Chin's offer of a large yearly bonus. Susan still looked after the injured and healthy animals but was unaware of the distribution arrangements. She believed they were just released back into the wild. Trevor was thankful he had no children. He was now complicit and mixed up in a business that could kill. On the bright side they had a limited identification footprint, and now had some bank savings and a couple of aging Landcruiser's, as well.

A year had gone by and Trevor was feeling increasingly worried that this whole endeavour would lead to gaol time or even death. Some of his animal collecting contacts suddenly disappeared when they wanted out. Susan was asking questions about his trips around the country, she was becoming suspicious. He had made up his mind that last October's raid on Rottnest Island was to be his last. He didn't want any part of this trade anymore, he never wanted to be in it in the first place.

Trevor had met a Chin associate who collected parrots from the Denmark area, he was an old bushy named Bob. He told Trevor he wouldn't be bringing in any more parrots. In a news report two weeks later, a man named Bob of no fixed address from the Denmark area, fell to his death at the Walpole *'Tree Top Walk'* in the Valley of the Giants. After that, Trevor knew that if he ever wanted out, he would have to go off the radar or face a similar fate.

Although Susan and Trevor had loved each other, their relationship was never a strong one. That night he came clean and told Susan the truth. She had a meltdown, screamed at him for his stupidity and cried herself to sleep. The next morning she had settled a bit, they discussed the possible murder of Bob and the problems with escaping the business. They both realised that finding a way out alive, may be impossible. Susan said she had had enough and she was leaving him. This came as a surprise to Trevor, he knew their marriage had issues, but he never realised she had it in her to just up and move back to her parent's place in Sydney. He was devastated, but he was aware she meant it, and would not return to him. It was then that he decided he would shut down the business now, while Chin was overseas and go off the radar.

Susan didn't muck around, within a week she had organised her few possessions, took half of their savings in cash and was driving the oldest Landcruiser across the Nullarbor to Sydney. When she arrived, she planned to leave the car in a suburban mall and catch a train to her parents' place. She left a paperless trail of her intended direction. Nobody, apart from Trevor knew her parents address or her maiden name, she was in the clear. Trevor was heartbroken, he thought deep down that their love for each other was two-way and despite this setback they would see it through together. He was wrong.

Trevor planned an escape that would, with a bit of luck, take a Hu Chin retribution out of the equation. He told neighbours and associates of his pending separation with Susan, and then packed all his remaining possessions into his Landcruiser. He told no-one of their plans. He would visit his mother in Gracetown and following this, he would drive to Broome and start a new life. He convinced himself that Susan would be safe in Sydney. Because of the animal shelters sudden shut down due to a marriage collapse, the threat of exposure of Rizky Lestari's criminal activity to authorities would be minimal. The fate of Hu Chin, although unfortunate, may hopefully be enough for Lestari to forget all about the Trussells and he would just have his Chinese Perth mates repossess the property.

A recent shipment of animals had been dispatched, and the shelter was at minimum capacity. Trevor was able to offload some of the remaining recuperating animals to other well-meaning carers in the area. He left a note on the door saying that he and Susan were having a weekend break in Bunbury. As usual he also said, your whisky is by the made-up trundle bed and there is food in the shelter fridge. He knew that after a long red-eye flight from Sydney that Chin would be tired. On his return to Perth, Chin always drove straight to the shelter to check up on the business. He would spend the night on a trundle bed with a bottle of Glenfiddich. By the time Chin decided he needed a sleep, Trevor would be halfway to Gracetown. Trevor never considered himself a cruel person, he loved most animals. Circumstances sometimes required that severely damaged creatures needed to be euthanised. He subconsciously told himself that this was one of those occasions. This eased his anxiety a little as he placed the open bag under the blanket at the base of the trundle bed.

Hu Chin arrived as expected, sneered at, and crumpled the door note. He then ate a salmon sandwich from the fridge, and in quick time sculled half the bottle of Glenfiddich. Three crushed Temaze sleeping tablets in the sandwich, swam with the whisky, and had Hu Chin dreaming of his future business empire within minutes. He didn't feel the juvenile western brown snake bite, and within six hours, as the sun rose on another fine day, he would never feel anything again.

* * *

Trevor Trussell arrived at his Gracetown home. He could hear Fart, the new family dog, barking in the backyard. Trevor found the house key in its normal spot under an old garden-gnome biscuit container on the porch. It held the ashes of several family pets. A cat called Muffin, a Parrott called Quokka and a wonderful kelpie called Goof. Goof was part of the family for eighteen years. When Trevor's mum and dad had the farm at Donnybrook, Goof could round up the few sheep they owned in minutes. When they made the sea change to Gracetown, old Goof did the same job with seagulls. His mum Gladys was always the tough one, the bad cop.

Trevor's dad, Brian, was always the good cop, and would often tell Trevor that his mum suffered from

I.T.I.S. Trevor would ask, "What's that?" and dad would answer, "intolerance to idiots syndrome son." That had the whole family laughing and being happy with life. The happiness fragmented for quite a while, when dad got hit and killed by lightning while fishing off Melaleuca Beach. Old Goof knew, he laid at mum's feet for months afterwards until she started ironing dad's clothes and swimming again. Old Goof died of natural causes a year later, he never returned. So, Gladys picked up another dog from the animal shelter. It was a young kelpie, it loved chasing seagulls as well. This pooch was always eating, it ate anything on offer. The trouble was it was always letting off wind and that would have Gladys running out the back door, she called the dog Fart.

Today was a perfect warm day, with; *'a few fluffy whites on a bright blue canvas.'* His dads weather descriptions always bought back great childhood memories. On the drive down he imagined his mum Gladys ironing his deceased dad's clothes, as if he was coming back home as soon as he had finished dying. His mum was always an optimist. Gladys wasn't home, and as expected neither was dad, he was taking a break at the Margaret River Cemetery. Trevor knew where to find his mum. Melaleuca Beach was the best place to go for a swim, so long as there were no shark sightings. Trevor dropped off his bags, * donned his budgies and boardies, grabbed a towel, and headed for the beach.

(C- *Aussie slang: He put on his speedo's and board shorts)

Trevor was still worried about outcomes, like Susan arriving safely in Sydney, and a certain snake performing its duty. At Melaleuca Beach the surf was still. There were a few people out swimming and he could see his mum not far from the shore. He had read about the washed-up shark and the unattached arm in the Freemantle Gazette. So, it was understandable that mum would be closer into shore. She was an optimist, but not a fool. Trevor jumped in the water and cooled off, it was instant worry relief. After the swim, Trevor and Gladys made their way to a nice warm spot in the sand. He chatted away about his recent exploits with the business and his sad separation with Susan.

"There's a strong smell of dead fish around here Mum. Was that shark incident near here somewhere?"

"Yes, I was here, they found an arm in its belly, I think we're sitting pretty close to the spot."

As he spoke, Trevor nervously dug the sand with his feet. He didn't want to tell his mum the whole truth about his involvement in the animal export extortion, nor what he hoped was the sad passing of Hu Chin. He had to keep some secrets in life. However, they did discuss his plans. Trevor told his mum he'd like to have a fresh start up at Broome. Gladys looked at him and said:

"Why not stay here son?"

"I just need a break; I need to get away and start a new life somewhere else. It's going to take some time to get over the disappointment of Susan leaving me. I'll stay here for a week or so, before I head off, we can have some fun and go swimming every day."

Gladys just smiled, she knew her son well. Trevor nervously dug around with his feet as he spoke and felt something like a chain wrap around his toe. He kicked it up, attached was a small leather pouch. He picked up the pouch and tipped the contents onto the towel.

(C...free at last!)

"Check this out mum, buried treasure, we're rich!' a cross, a ring, and a coin."

"I wonder if that came out of the sharks belly son?"

"I suppose it could have, but it would be impossible to prove who owned it. I might post the cross to Susan, she is a good Catholic girl. I will keep the two bucks and the ring. You never know I might meet someone new one day."

Trevor frowned at that thought, he missed Susan and he felt a bit unfaithful. Gladys picked up on his sudden mood swing. He placed the broken chain in the pouch and sat sullen for a moment.

"Life is like a box of chocolates Forest," she said, and they both had a laugh.

Trevor then noticed the coins inscription; '*love is a currency spend it wisely*'. He looked at Gladys and read the inscription as a tear welled in his eye. She just stared at him and said, "that's got to hurt son."

"I guess I haven't been too wise lately mum."

"Remember what dad use to say Trevor, '*they can't teach wisdom, only living does that,*' Let's go and have some lunch, your father might be home by now."

Trevor just looked at his mum with love in his eyes, as Fart ran by, chasing a seagull.

CHAPTER 6... THE ROAD TO ALBANY

After the exciting great white shark encounter at Gracetown, Horace Winterbottom continued his trip south to Augusta, the toe of Australia. He stopped at what an English man calls a Chippy, it was named the *'Crab-Claw Café.'* It was near the Augusta information centre. Naturally, Horace ordered a 'crab-claw-rissole' sandwich, the house specialty. The owner, a friendly guy called Gus Cook joked about Horace's attire:

"Where's the funeral mate?"

Horace had a chuckle at the man's surname, and was starting to get used to Aussie humour. He came back with:

"Wasn't he a friend of yours?"

This shook Gus for a second, until Horace smiled. He then noticed that Gus had trinkets for sale. A small plastic Blue Swimmer crab, mounted on a piece of a Jarrah tree with a message. *'Enjoy your crabby time in Augusta.'*

It was just the trinket Horace wanted for his collectable memories in his vintage school case. This purchase prompted a lengthy conversation about life in Augusta, crab pots and crab claw rissoles that don't nip. Gus told Horace that the best place to stay for a night was the back packers opposite the Augusta pub. Horace thanked him and Gus had the last word:

"As a bonus they don't have crabs there!"

Horace thought about that for a second, then

laughed and waved goodbye.

Cape Leeuwin Lighthouse was Augusta's biggest tourist attraction. It was the closest Horace would ever get to Antarctica. It also provided a wonderful opportunity to sit and ponder on his adventure so far. It was a calm day and the ocean was as still as an English bath. Horace planned to write two postcards; both will share the same shark stories. There were a few tourists at the fence adjacent to the lighthouse. As usual, Horace looked like a casual funeral director, cuffs up to the knees and shirt sleeves to his elbows.

A tall lean sunburnt Australian with a well-worn tattoo on his wrist, said g'day mate. Horace read the name on the wrist as Sultana-Bran. He wasn't sure if that was the blokes name or his favourite fruit cereal, so he just acknowledged him with a nod. He then stepped over the fence, which was adjacent to a warning sign about dangerous surf. As he made his way to a quiet spot at the water's edge, Horace almost tripped on an orange life boy that was secured in place to rescue stupid tourists. He sat there with his feet in the water writing the postcards. The salt air was invigorating, he was feeling like he was sitting on the edge of the world. He had his left foot in the Great Southern Ocean, and his right foot in the Indian Ocean.

As he wrote the postcards, a small Blue Swimmer crab washed by, saw a tasty white worm, and nipped Horace's right pinkie toe. Horace jumped up in shock and almost fell into the Indian Ocean. He turned around and saw Sultana laughing at him:

"It's a long swim home from there mate, especially in that clobber!"

Horace, although embarrassed, could see the humour, and waved with a broad Pommy smile. He then limped back to the car and drove to the back packer accommodation.

After a rest, it was late afternoon, and Horace needed a beer. He walked across the road to the Augusta pub, he could hear a guitar and harmonica. They were in sync with the laconic twang of a country singer. The words were sad, about a jilted lover, a girl named Bron, and a dog named Speed.

The entertainment poster said:

'Appearing tonight for one night only, a trip down memory lane with our special guest country boy Chilli-Jam Johnson'.

Horace walked in and saw that Sultana-Bran was holding the guitar with a harmonica around his neck.

＊ ＊ ＊

Back in the 1970s Chilli-Jam Johnson was a knockabout country rocker in outback New South Wales. He had made some cool sounds with his guitar, harmonica, and raspy voice. Some of his songs were extremely popular, so he had produced a few records. He had a look about him that hadn't changed in fifty-years, with a mullet haircut, his wardrobe of a dozen black Santana tee-shirts and well-worn denim jeans. This look was finished off with white braces and a Ford V-8 belt buckle. His real name was Charles Johnson and he fell in love with a groupie who followed him around to most venues. Her name was Bronwyn Tucker, Chilli called her Bron, she left home in Brisbane at the age of sixteen and was still on a missing persons list. Chilli's life loves were Santana and Bron, so he had their names tattooed on his inner left arm.

Chilli and Bron went through a bad patch in the early eighties. They were both addicted to weed, and then moved on to heavier drugs. He drank and shot up almost all his earnings. His voice even started to fail him. It was at the Tamworth music festival that things hit the wall. He was booed off stage and Bron injected a little too much. After her pauper's funeral, Chilli tried to clean himself up a little. He hung up his guitar and got a second job as a drover. He grew up on an outback station and knew his way around horses and spent the next twenty years out in the sun for days on end. His skin was now weathered, his hair discovered gravity before it went white, and his well-worn Akubra hat covered the bald spots. The good news was his singing voice came back with an even gravellier tone.

He gave up the droving life and hit the music highway again, writing his personal sad love songs from life experiences. This got him doing gigs again in pubs around the country. Chilli was accustomed to sleeping outdoors with his swag, and only occasionally spent the nights in pubs. He moved around the country by train, hitch hiking or on foot. One day he was making his way to the main pub in Dunedoo when an under fed cattle dog started to follow him. It walked really slow with its head down and tongue out. Chilli stopped and gave the dog a drink and half a ham sandwich he had in his kit. That dog became his next life love, it followed him everywhere, although very slowly. Chilli named him Speed; they were best of mates.

Speed would sit on the verandas of the pubs and

listened to his master sing. Every now and then he would hear his name in a song and poke his head in the door. Chilli still loved a beer, and the only drugs he had these days were for cholesterol and blood pressure. The karaoke nights were his favourite, the tips were so good. The aging years in the sun had weathered Chilli's body. This combined with droving scars and branding burns had played havoc with his tattoos. His true loves were now exposed as Sultana-Bran. It didn't bother him much, but when he strummed his guitar, his left arm faced the audience, and he copped a barrage of cereal jokes.

❋ ❋ ❋

Chilli finished his first set in the Augusta pub, and saw the bloke in the bowler hat walk in. He went over to where Horace sat.

"Ok if I sit here mate?"

"Yes, by all means lad"

Horace loved talking to people, it was all material for his travel diary. This fellow had a look about him that cried out interest. Horace bought a round of schooners and Chilli asked a few questions about Horace's journey; it was obvious he was a tourist. Horace told him he was a travel writer for 'Finding Earth Magazine,' making his way around Australia and visiting places off the normal tourist routes, where possible.

"I noticed your name is not Sultana-Bran, it's Chilli-Jam?"

"Yes, just don't call me Cereal, I cop that regularly these days."

"I was also called Chilli at school, Chilli-ass actually,

names Horace Winterbottom, pleased to meet you."

They both had a chuckle, and Chilli gave him a brief rundown of his life.

"Heard your song about Bron and Speed, it's a sad tale of her demise, but what happened to Speed?"

"Well, that's a sad tale too. It's the reason I left the outback and came over here. I needed a change after losing Speed, another dog was biting me, and it was black, depression has no master. Speed was a great dog, he helped me get over some of the rubbish life throws to trip you up. I had a gig at Pinky's Roadhouse in Oodnadatta, and I left Speed on the veranda, as per usual. Some of the patrons knew the story of him poking his head in the door when his name came up in a song. They always turned to look at the door when I sung his name, it became a bit of a tradition."

Chilli continued with the tale, while Horace sat there absorbed by every word.

"There was a story about him in the paper, which was great for me and my work. On this occasion, Speed didn't look just at me he stared at the crowd, barked once, and disappeared. He was getting on in age, a lot slower, and he was dragging his feet a little. Looking back now, I believe he knew his time was up. After the show, I couldn't find him, and some of the locals helped me search. He was found curled up under one of the few trees in town, adjacent the roadhouse. It broke my heart. The locals helped me bury him at the foot of the tree. Just before I left town, someone had nailed a board on the tree, with the words, 'Speed, the slow dog of song, he never put a paw wrong.' It was a fitting tribute to my best mate."

They sat there in a thought bubble, both sad for a

moment, then Chilli went back to the stage. After his last set, Chilli came back to the table with two beers.

"Where are you heading next Chilli?"

"I'm travelling north on the inland route. I don't normally drive, thumbed most of my way through life, but out here you need a car. I picked up an old holden Ute in Bunbury, it'll get me there. I've got a one-nighter at the Commercial Hotel in Meekatharra and then two nights at the Walkabout Hotel in Port Headland. Flat country, barely any trees and hot. It's no wonder the bloody Dutch turned their noses up at the joint. After that the Roebuck Bay Pub in Broome, and a hop skip and a jump to Darwin, with hope to strum my way there, nothing booked. What about you?"

"I'm going to check out Albany, there is a statue of Ataturk looking back to Gallipoli at the war museum. I read up on the Australian Light Horse Brigade, who left from there in the first world war. I also hope to see a blue whale swim by, and I want to do the tree top walk in Walpole. After that I might make my way to Broome as well, One Earth gave me free reign."

"Cheers to you Horace, we may cross paths again one day. By the way mate, do yourself a favour, get some new clobber before you roast to death in the north. Don't forget summer is coming and that means rain and heat. Out here you need shorts, a tee-shirt, and thongs. And that silly pot on your head needs a bigger brim."

Chilli had a chuckle as Horace got up to leave:

"Thanks for the free advice lad, it's been great chatting. But I won't be wearing any thongs, I've been told they chafe your bum."

Chilli left to pack his gear smiling. He felt a little

bit of the black-dog fade. Horace waved as he crossed the road, he had another great yarn for the diary. A thought crossed his mind, he would have some Sultana Bran for breakfast.

The next day Horace was in an adventurous travel mood. He stopped at Walpole, the area is best known for the *'Valley of the Giants'*, where huge red tingle trees grow. Horace could have driven his car through one of the trees, they were that big. He walked on the famous *'Tree Top Walk'*, fourty metres above the forest floor and had a birds-eye view of the forest below. Horace recently read in a newspaper article that a local fell to his death from this same spot not long ago. He noted that he should be careful but was very impressed with the vista.

After the walk he needed a cuppa. There was an Australian wildlife enclosure around the café. It included Wallaroos, Quolls, Potoroos and Quokkas, but they were hard to see, mostly being nocturnal. The ever-chatty Horace sat down opposite and started up a conversation with two American tourists, named Shane and Clarissa Huckster. They were dressed like National Park guides, walking boots, wicking shirts, and pants, with all the trims. They had Swiss army knives in leather scabbards, and each had fancy looking water bottles in special pouches on their day packs. They looked like they were off on a Kathmandu adventure. Horace sized then up, he thought there was something more to this pair. He was looking at their matching water bottles.

"Those bottles look special, whiskey or water?" He laughed.

Shane responded with an air of indifference. "No just water, we walk a lot."

"They don't look shop bought?"

"No, they were an anniversary gift from a friend in Africa, he had them specially made in Switzerland."

The Hucksters were world travellers from Boston and were heading to Esperance and the Nullarbor on an around Australia journey. Horace was amazed to hear of their travels. They told him they had made their wealth in jewellery and were now enjoying the rewards of retirement. They had recently flown in from Africa and had seen many animals over there on a safari through Botswana. As they spoke, a creature dubbed the world's happiest animal, hopped up, it was a cute quokka.

"Wow!" Said Shane, "I just read about these little guys. A Chinese chap was found dead in an animal shelter south of Fremantle. Border Force said he was suspected of participating in the exotic animal trade and specialised in Quokkas. It seems he got his just desserts, the paper headline pun read, 'Australia bites back', he was bitten by a snake while sleeping. The police are now worried about the owners of the shelter, they are missing. There was a fire at the shelter a week after the body was found. It was said to be caused by an electrical fault; the whole place was gutted."

Horace was listening intently and made a note to research Quokkas and rich American jewellery merchants. This country was full of surprises. He wanted a little bit more information on this family, something was ringing bells in his journalistic mind. So, he offered them his business card. It was a simple card with a Derby Bowler hat picture, his name and the company 'Finding Earth Magazine', plus their Web address. In return Shane offered his card, it too was straight forward. Their names, an American phone number, and a picture of a large cut diamond. Horace quoted, in his Shakespearian way, from Henry V1,

'My Crown is in my heart, not on my head, and not decked with diamonds'.

He then smiled and bid farewell to these Americans. Shane and Clarissa laughed. Clarissa had the last words:

"Lovely to meet you Horace, if you're ever in Boston give us a ring, it would be great to hear about your travels".

On the way out of the Café Horace purchased a small Quokka soft toy, for his vintage school case. Sadly, it was made in China, he then continued his journey.

❊ ❊ ❊

Unknown to Horace, Shane and Clarissa Huckster were not your usual American tourists. They were in fact high end traffickers for a world criminal syndicate. Their trip to Botswana was more about diamonds than animal safaris. Botswana is one of the most politically stable countries in Africa, and it is the second largest producer of conflict-free diamonds. Diamond smugglers infiltrate the country and they are aided by locals. A Botswana criminal syndicate known as Larona-pula, had world contacts for their illegal diamond exports. Tebogo Modise was the head guy in Larona-pula, he lived in the capital Gaborone. The Hucksters were there for more than safaris.

Recently an enormous one thousand plus carat diamond was unearthed by a mining company at the Karori diamond mine. It was said to be the fourth most massive diamond found in the country in the space of a few weeks. The truth was that there were three such similar stones discovered at that site, at that time. Two of the rare rocks found their way via the local workers network into the hands of Tebogo. The remaining diamond was presented to the government in a ceremony, the Governor stated:

"It should fetch around $40 million and benefit all Botswanans".

Tebogo often went to the Gaborone Yacht Club to meet business contacts. The Hucksters had been there to collect, and then carry the stones through customs, and eventually to a dealer in New York. Their water bottles had secret compartments at the base and had successfully been through many scanners over the years. The fees on delivery were substantial.

* * *

Horace arrived in Albany, had a haircut, and went shopping. Following Chilli's advice, he bought some shorts, jeans, polar tops, and a wind jacket. It wasn't English weather here, but still a bit cool on spring mornings. He didn't mention the thongs to the shop assistant, but he did buy some walking shoes and some long socks. He felt pleased with the purchase, and he walked out of the shop carrying the suit back to the motel, wearing the new clobber. Horace thought he was now dressed for the climate, but he still looked like an English tourist. His shirt was tucked into his jeans, he had a thin black belt and the pants road high above his belly button. The top button of his shirt was done up and he wore the bright yellow wind jacket. It was all an improvement on the funeral outfit, but people walking by still stared at the bowler hat sitting on top.

Albany was everything that Horace had expected. The vintage school case had another memory. After visiting the Ataturk statue, the museum and buying a book on the horse stories of the Light-Horsemen, he went for a drive to the famous Two Peoples National Park. It was a still bright day without a cloud. The sand was white and the water was exceptionally blue. It was low tide, and a large granite boulder was the centrepiece of a magic outlook over the Great Southern Ocean. Horace had brought with him a packed lunch and a thermos of coffee. He was alone on the beach and sat there on the boulder for two hours just taking in the ambiance of one of the quietest places on earth. Horace looked out on the ocean, and he was thrilled to behold the spray of a large whale. Its body was huge as it rolled through the waves. He realised he was watching a blue whale in motion. It went in his diary as one of the highlights of his life.

On the way back to Perth he stopped at the 'Thirsty Camel' in Denmark. It was appropriately named. Horace was quite in need of an ale and lunch after the long drive. While parking the car he noticed a large contingent of motorbikes. The public bar was full of aging retired men with wrinkled cheeks and white beards. They were all wearing ear and nose rings, and black leather. By the look of their jacket logos, they were called the 'Great Australian Blight.' Every eye in the pub followed Horace across the room. He thought that his green belt in judo would be useless here. So, he placed his hat on the bar and smiled at the room.

In true English form he ordered a *'Ploughman's Lunch,'* but had to settle with a burger and chips. The cold schooner of beer came next, and that quelled some of his anxiety. He sat at the bar next to a large fellow wearing a black tee-shirt with white writing on it. To Horace it was quite a truthful statement, apart from the spelling, it read; *'Mozzys Love Blood'*. All the other chap's arms, legs, and faces were covered in various tattoos, but what got Horace's attention was the *'Grim Reaper'* on all their arms. He introduced himself to the man next to him at the bar, his name was Mozzy:

"Well that is a coincidence", thought Horace.

Mozzy just stared at Horace; he was trying not to laugh.

'What the hell is this bloke about?', he thought.

Horace was so out of place here. He was like a lamb chop in a pride of old lions. Lucky for him he didn't see it that way, and neither did the top lion.

"What's with the hat?" Mozzy asked.

"Keeps my balding head from burning."

"It needs a bigger brim around here mate!" he laughed.

Horace continued to eat, the other bikers lost interest, and continued with their conversations. He finished the burger and gulped down a mouthful of beer. He then looked at Mozzy, and with the tact of a British hospice matron said:

"I've seen that Grim Reaper tattoo on your arm before lad, it recently slipped out of a shark's belly at Gracetown beach."

"You were there?" sparked Mozzy.

"Yes, it was a rather gruesome moment."

"He was one of our bike riders, we are a tribe.' Mozzy bowed his head a little, with a sullen look on his face.

With the use of the word tribe, Horace thought *'how anachronistic,'* but he showed some empathy on his face. Deep down he now glowed with a touch of excitement. He was thinking that this encounter was a chance to '*dot some I's and cross some T's'* in a good story.

"I will bet there's a sad tale here. How did the arm of your mate end up in a shark's belly?"

"There is not really a lot of information," said Mozzy. "Ajax was a loner, with anger issues and he left us in Esperance. The last time we spoke he was sitting in a shopping centre gutter, next to a broken koala piggy bank. He had blood on his ear and was as cranky as bees in a disturbed hive."

"Did you just say a broken koala piggy bank!" exclaimed Horace.

"Yeah, some local Aboriginal chucked it at him, out of a passing car."

Horace was even more intrigued. *'Crazy!'* He thought, *'what are the chances that it was the one he swapped for the boomerang'*

Mozzy continued. "It was the last time we spoke. The *'Grim Reaper'* tattoo led the coppers to us. When they contacted me, I was told that Ajax was booked in for a shark dive off Cull Island, and he disappeared from the cage. The owner, a bloke named Burlington, claimed the shark didn't take him. They were thinking he had a medical episode and drifted off in the current. The swallowed arm was just a post shark snack on a corpse."

"How did they know it was Ajax's arm?"

"It's the only one we have lost in recent years, it had to be Ajax."

All the other bikers overheard the conversation and were staring at Mozzy. A bloke called Boil stepped out of the group and raised his beer; "To Ajax!" he yelled. The group followed the tribute, as did Horace. He chatted with Mozzy after the toast about the tribe, and where they were heading.

"Cable beach, Broome for a sunset Camel ride," said Mozzy.

"Well, that's a coincidence, I'm heading there as well, we might catch up on the road, or perhaps in a village inn."

Horace left the bar with a cryptic smile and in two minds, whether he should drive to Esperance for a shark story chat with this Mr Burlington or just ring. He decided on the latter. Horace was also thinking about the koala piggy bank, he loved coincidence and chance, so he decided to call Nancy Coogan in Kalgoorlie as well.

CHAPTER 7... THE ROAD TO BROOME

When Rizky Lestari learnt the fate of Hu Chin, he was not a happy crime boss. He had agents check out three other West Australian Trevor Trussells on Facebook to no avail. The trail on Trevor's wife Susan had also gone cold. They were now checking hotels and towns on all roads out of Perth. Trevor was off the grid and Hu Chin's knowledge and memories of the Trussells was still smouldering in the remains of the Oldbury shelter. The insurance on the shelter and the sale of the land would provide some recompense for Rizky, but other avenues of exotic animals would have to be found. Rizky was now aware of the Border Force investigations and would have to shut the whole operation down for a while. He wanted a blood payment for the inconvenience, that blood was to be Trevor Trussells.

※ ※ ※

There are more than fifty towns in Western Australia whose names ended in UP, its Aboriginal meaning is *'place'*. Horace didn't like long drives; two hours was too long. So, he took the inland route back to Perth and found a cabin at a place called Kojonup, translation stone-axe-place. He made his calls there.

Ethan Burlington had been short on detail about Ajax when Horace finally managed to track him down. All he said was that:

"Ajax was a quiet bloke and short on conversation."

Horace thought the guy may have been worried that he was someone from the world of red tape. He felt fobbed off, but he had more luck with Nancy Coogan in Kalgoorlie.

'It's a staggering coincidence,' thought Horace. *'An Aboriginal seen running from the pub, holding a koala piggy bank, it had to be the same one, wow!'*

Horace just got off the phone to Nancy, she suspected a bloke named *'Walkabout Jimmy'* had flogged it, and he probably came back for that boomerang they had exchanged.

Horace was amazed, *'that koala found its way to an altercation with a bikie in Esperance, life is certainly strange'.*

Kojonup was a friendly village. Horace had a chicken pizza for dinner and then crossed the road to the Royal Hotel. It was noticeably quiet, there was a young barmaid, two guys playing pool and an old guy sipping on a beer at the far end of the bar. Horace heard a car pull up out the front, they skidded to a stop and marched into the pub holding a picture. They were two Asian businessmen, and they looked serious. They showed the picture to the barmaid, the pool players and the old guy, all heads were nodding no. Horace was next, when they saw him, they hesitated, he was back in the funeral director outfit. They showed him the picture and asked in broken English with a direct unfriendly manner:

"You see this fellow round here?"

"What's his name?"

"Why you ask?"

"I'm better with names than faces." He lied; Horace was now sensing a rudeness that annoyed him.

"He name Trevor Trussell, you know him, you see him round here?"

"Is that Trussell, with SSs not ZZ's?"

"What it matter?"

"It does to some." Smirked Horace, "No I don't know him, nor have I seen him."

The men just sneered at Horace, walked off, jumped in the car, and skidded off down the road.

"Well, that was strange," said the barmaid to no one in particular.

Horace was remembering his encounter with Gladys Trussell, 'with SS's not ZZ's', she said, if he was to include her name in a magazine article. He was now thinking how she would have managed these thugs. 'That would be a great show to watch.' He was also puzzled about the reason. Finding one special Trussell in Western Australia would be as hard as finding Lasseter's famed reef of gold.

'I wonder if they tried Google or a phone book?' Horace laughed to himself at the thought. The next day after successfully buying an imitation stone axe head from the local antique shop, he headed off to Perth. His school case was filling fast.

* * *

Gladys Trussell had just finished re-ironing her husband's clothes and was heading out the door to go shopping when a car pulled up out the front. A young

Chinese gentleman hopped out, he was quite polite and introduced himself.

"Hi, I'm Han, a friend of Trevor's, is he around?"

He said this with a confident smile. Gladys was no fool, the world is full of salesmen, so she remained coy:

"Where do you know Trevor from?" she asked.

At this stage Han was not aware if there was any connexion between this lady and Trevor, but she was the only Trussell in the area, and it was worth the gamble.

"Oh, I've known Trevor and Susan for years and I heard about their breakup. I was in the area and thought he might head down here."

Han's little trick paid off, Gladys took the bait and answered him, her suspicious demeanour changed a bit with the mention of the breakup.

"Trevor is not here now; he left for Broome a few days ago."

"Oh, that's a shame," said Han, "I was looking forward to catching up."

Suddenly, Han's friendly disposition changed, he said nothing more, jumped in the car and drove off. With this action Gladys became extremely worried.

"I hope Trevor is not in any kind of trouble," she thought, and wished her departed husband Brian would come home soon.

* * *

Trevor Trussell was sitting at the bar at the Walkabout pub in Port Headland, listening to a country singer ranting sad tales of woe. Trevor was also feeling low, he took out the leather pouch and tipped the contents onto the bar. The cross followed the ring and the coin. The coin rolled down the bar, *(C...here we go again)*, and onto the floor near the stage. Trevor ignored it, the loss of a coin and its message of wise love brought back too many sad memories. He looked at the cross and the ring, both were symbols of a church wedding, and again he thought of Susan. She was Catholic, so he decided to post it to her parent's place with a letter of his feelings towards her. He was now missing her greatly. The ring he would keep, if things didn't work out in the future, he might find another love in his life. Trevor had recently read in the paper about Hu Chin being discovered and realised that the police were looking for him. He was not in any hurry to be found, he had cash and enough to live on for quite some time.

There was a lady sitting near the stage, glue eyed on Chilli, and smitten by his sad words. She was trying to capture his attention with a smile. Her name was Veronica Cullen. She caught the glint of the coin as it fell from the bar, and she had no idea where it came from. It landed near her foot, she reached down and picked it up and read the inscription. It was a shock and brought an attractive grin to her face. As she looked back at the stage Chilli was smiling at her, it was an omen of pending romance. Veronica was a young-looking 50-year-old, married twice to low-life bullies who loved bashing her. She finally escaped, bought a Campervan, and hit the road.

Veronica and Chilli hit it off from first sight, it was more than just a one-night stand. As it turned out they both needed new love in their life. It was time to move on, she had found a kind man, and he had found a woman with no attachments, who just needed to be respected. It wasn't a challenge for either. They had like interests in relation to where they wanted to be and that was nowhere in particular.

So, after the second night in Port Hedland, Veronica suggested:

"Why not hitch a ride with me, sell that old bomb, and we'll see where the road leads us."

Chilli's thoughts sparkled, *'why not.'* The prospect was great, apart from having company, he had someone to share the driving and fuel costs. He could tell she was a good woman, and she knew how to laugh. They hit the road to Broome, not worried about their future, or the past. Veronica's thoughts went back to the coin that dropped near her foot, *'love is a currency spend it wisely,'* and that is what she would do from now on. She dropped the coin into the console of the campervan and drove on.

(C... it was a bumpy ride, but most lives are)

* * *

Horace didn't stay to visit Perth; he had been there and done that before. He just checked into a cheap motel, had a chat at an adjacent pub with a local real estate agent he recognised, and checked out after breakfast. The temperature was now rising, the further he headed north the warmer it got. The next night he spent in Julien; nothing fancy there. It was flat and dull, apart from the sky. The clouds were weird, they were white and feathery like a jihad of giant cockies had been in a scuffle. By the time Horace arrived in Geraldton it was time to shed the jeans. He had donned his shorts and his socks were pulled up above his calves, in a new *'Mr Bean'* plays golf look.

After Geraldton, Horace was still more than two thousand kilometres from Broome:

'My goodness this is a big country.'

He had to rethink his road time. He increased it to roughly four hourly trips, which meant about six stops, and hopefully stories, before that sunset camel ride. Another adventure on his bucket list, was at Shark Bay.

'I just must swim with a dolphin at Monkey Mia.

Horace thought ahead and booked his stay at the World Heritage listed Shark Bay. It was a tourist spot and visiting Monkey Mia for a dolphin experience was extremely popular. Originally, people would just camp here, swim with, and feed the friendly dolphins, cost free. Naturally these days an entry-fee had to be paid to enter any of the reserves. The dolphin interaction was free, but the rangers on duty would only allow feeding, not swimming. *'Popularity sometimes sucked'*, thought Horace. He asked around and found a place not far from the no touching, no swimming experience. In a convenient public change room and toilet, Horace donned his budgie smugglers and had his own personal dolphin encounter.

He was in clear water up to his belly button when it happened. He thought his chances were limited at this site, most of the paid dolphins earned their fish around the corner, but this big fellow came floating past and gave Horace the one eyed once over. It must have been curious of the Derby Bowler still on Horace's head. When he looked back to the beach, there was a lady staring in his direction jumping up and down and clapping.

After the short paddle, he introduced himself and

chatted to this lovely Japanese lady, her name was Waiehu Sakura, she was the happy beach clapper. She told him she was excited for him; she had been there all morning and not seen one dolphin:

"It must have been waiting for you."

At that instant other dolphins arrived which just added to her excitement. They watched these dolphins behaving naturally, while they talked about their travels. Waiehu told Horace that her great grandfather was a pearl diver at Broome before the war. Horace found her to be a wealth of knowledge. He also found out that Mia is the Aboriginal term for home, and the Monkey part of the local name is allegedly derived from a pearling boat called the Monkey. It had anchored here in the late nineteenth century, during the days when pearling was an industry in the region. She also gave him the story of dolphin's misogynistic behaviour, which rivalled that of some politicians.

"It seems that gangs of male dolphins may isolate a defenceless female, slap her around with their tails, and forcibly copulate with her for weeks. It is not all bad news," she said with a giggle, "female dolphins have orgasms too, they're basically ocean nymphomaniacs."

Horace was so stunned with that; he almost fell over.

"Well, I'm certainly glad that the big male I encountered didn't mistake me for a weird looking female."

Waiehu was laughing at his humour as they walked off the beach.

On the way back to the change room, Waiehu told Horace that she was originally from Fujiyama in Japan, and now a postgraduate in marine biology on an around Australia sabbatical. This was all prior to taking up a position with the University of Queensland for research on a Barrier Reef Island. She spoke in clear refined English with only a hint of an accent. Her other reason for coming to this location was to visit the oldest known life forms on Earth, the remarkable Hamelin Pool Stromatolites. This really captured Horace's attention. He told her that he had seen Thrombolite steppingstones at Lake Clifton.

"Yes, these microbial giants are the Thrombolite cousins. They're not far from here Horace, about an hour and a half drive and on the way back to the Coral Coast Road. Stromatolites were likely the first living organisms on Earth, with fossil records dating back 3.7 billion years. Today, stromatolites are rare, mostly existing in fossil form but the Stromatolites growing at Hamelin Pool are alive. The sea water here is twice as salty as normal sea water. There is a sand bar across the entrance of the bay and the salt builds up due to the rapid evaporation of the shallow water. Did you know Horace, the reason there is so much iron ore around this region is because the Stromatolites ancestors produced the first oxygen on Earth."

(C...suck it up, a little education won't kill you)

Horace was flummoxed, this woman was a walking encyclopedia. The next day he followed her to Hamelin Pools. It was a surreal experience for them both.

"Time traveling is always fun," said Horace, as they exchanged phone contact details and parted ways. He had a strong inclination that their paths would cross again. At this stage of his odyssey, the vintage school case was filling fast, but it still had room for pub coasters and monogrammed beer coolers. The last two coolers had pictures of Monkey Mia dolphins and ancient Stromatolites. He still wanted to find a replacement koala piggy bank.

The remainder of Horace's journey north to Broome was unremarkable. Carnarvon was pleasant and had some interesting aspects. From there driving safely became the main objective. There wasn't much to see, other than; orange sand dunes, tufts of faded green shrubs and a wide blue ocean. The best part of the journey were the sunsets, they were remarkable. He passed through Karratha and Port Headland, and nothing grabbed his attention, it was very industrial. Piles of iron ore and other Australian mineral resources were being shipped off to faraway places. There were large trucks, large machinery, and large men all working in the heat and dust. He had some stories, gathered from people who were only there for the money and who were obviously homesick. The permanents were generally store owners, diehard red necks, back-packers, and Aboriginals, all who talked of tough times, good times, cyclones, and country.

CHAPTER 8... SUNSET CONJUNCTION

In July 1992 a large U.N peacekeeping force was deployed into Somalia. Factional fighting and the absence of a central government led the country to being called a failed state. During this tragic time, one young woman on the outskirts of Mogadishu was raped by a gang of retreating militia. She managed to escape the group and made her way to an uncle's farm west of the city. It was here that she gave birth to triplets. The three brothers she named Zahi, Taifa and Axmed. They grew up poor and tough and eventually fled to Botswana. Their uncle's friend in Gaborone was an up-and-coming criminal named Tebogo Modise. Under his mentorship they were at first educated and then trained in combat. They grew into educated killers and graduated into Tebogo's growing Botswana criminal syndicate called Larona-pula.

The trade in illegal diamonds was very profitable. When the trio turned eighteen Tebogo gave them each a handcrafted Damascus steel Bowie knife. The trio became mercenaries for hire. Their knife skills were weaponised and their brotherly bonding a force to be feared. Within this dark-web world of crime, they were known as the 'Lions of Mogadishu'. An Indonesian acquaintance of Tebogo was an unscrupulous criminal named Rizky Lestari. He was in a different illegal trade, that involved animals, but from time to time he used Tebogo's human resources. Larona-pula also assisted Rizky in certain

African animal transactions and extractions.

All three of the *'Lions of Mogadishu'* were currently in Australia for varied reasons. Zahi and Taifa were on the East Coast on a surveillance mission of competitive forces in Tobogo's trade. Axmed was on the West coast for the same reason. A call from Listari to Tobogo had Axmed dispatched to Broome, for an unrelated mission.

✽ ✽ ✽

Trevor Trussell was no tourist, he drove to Broome on the direct route, only stopping on three occasions. It didn't take him long to find accommodation, he wasn't fussy. He secured a partly furnished one bedroom flat in Dampier Street, not far from the famous Roebuck pub and the Pearl luggers. He was in no hurry to find work and decided to spend a few weeks getting to know the place and seeing the sights. For the time being he signed himself in as Sam Brown and paid a cash deposit. The agents in Broome were laid back and they didn't concern themselves with people's history, just their ability to pay.

✽ ✽ ✽

When Horace finally arrived in Broome, he was exhausted and needed a beer. The Roebuck Hotel assumed a fair slice of the town. He imagined pearl divers and salty sailors tramping seaweed and red dust through here back in the nineteenth century. He made this spot his first port of call for accommodation and a shower, which would help wash away the red dust and fly dung. After that, he dressed like a local, *(C...or so he thought)* and headed for the Roey sports bar for a well-earned beer.

As he sat there drinking his beer, he was suddenly stunned by an horrific noise from outside. He looked out the window and thought a plane was about to join him for dinner. It was heading towards the Main Street of Broome. Nobody else in the bar flinched, it turned out that people from Broome don't like to walk far to catch a plane. The airport runway was across the street from the main shopping thoroughfare. Thankfully planes land here infrequently. Horace imagined that the locals got used to the noise. As he looked out the window towards the descending plane, a fella walked past on the opposite side of the street. Horace had a recollection of the face; it was the bloke in the photograph the two rude Asians showed him in Kojonup. He didn't give it another thought for a while and ordered himself a steak and chips from the bar, while he caught up with a bit of news on the television. It was about an hour later when the chap walked into the bar. At about this time Horace heard music coming from the main hotel and he recognised the singer. His old mate from Augusta, Chilli Jam, was depressing locals with song.

Horace was getting up to leave and say hello to Chilli in the other bar when the person from the photograph stood up and brushed past him. Horace could see a story here and started up a conversation about the aircraft noise.

"That plane gave me a bit of a fright, thought it was going to land on the bar."

"Yes, I had the same thought when I arrived as well."

Trevor introduced himself as Sam Brown, and he was keen for a bit of conversation. It becomes lonely after a while when you're trying to stay inconspicuous. Trevor thought that this strange Englishman seemed harmless enough. They had a beer shout each and talked for a while about the weather and outback travel. After a few beers Horace always became friendlier and decided to tell this person about the photo.

"I've seen you before Sam"

"Where abouts?"

"Two rude Asian fellows in Kojonup showed me a picture of you and called you Trevor Trussell."

Trevor started to shake a little and fear clouded his face:

"They're looking for me, shit, I'm a dead man walking."

Horace tried to settle him a bit, "they wouldn't find you way up here, surely. Do I call you Trevor?"

"Yes, it's me, you found me, they probably will eventually as well."

"They looked like bad people, maybe you should go to the Police."

"No, these people won't rest, I'll hang around here a bit and move on."

"It's funny you know I had never heard of the name Trussell before, and since I arrived in Western Australia, I've met two. Just a few weeks ago, a lady on the beach at Gracetown introduced herself as Gladys Trussell."

Trevor just stared at him, sick to the stomach, "that's my mum."

With that bit of news Trevor began to think that Rizky Lestari's thugs may track him down quicker than he thought. He thanked Horace for the information and walked out the door. Horace noticed a big African man sitting on the other side of the room get up to leave as well and follow Trevor out the door. Horace didn't like to get involved in things where he may end up in danger, bravery wasn't one of his strong points. He had suspicions about this fellow and thought he would warn Trevor. He finished his beer and walked out onto Dampier Terrace, then followed them for a bit. Trevor turned into a tree lined alley, as did the big African bloke.

Axmed, knew what he was doing, a quick kill was a good kill. There was no need for this animal to suffer more than necessary. The mission was to take him out and then get out, with a minimum of fuss. There was a boat ready to go that would drop him off at a quiet port in the south where he would remain until things settled. He drew his Bowie knife, which was honed to perfection and attacked with the skill of a vicious lion.

Horace ran to catch up. Suddenly there was this cacophony of noise, he thought another plane was about to land in the car park at the end of the alley. He called out, but it was too late, Trevor was pinned up against a tree and a large knife was being plunged into his stomach. The killer then looked at Horace, he was a witness, and he would be next. Horace realised his green belt in judo would be useless once again, he was in serious danger. His brain was calling out fight or flight, it chose the latter. All he could do was run. His bowler hat took to the sky, and he stumbled over a tree root. He was on his stomach when the thug caught him, Horace braced himself for pain. Suddenly, he was free, a large foot had collected the would-be killer, it winded Axmed. He was then shoved across the alley, then another boot went into his ribs. The attacker, who was as big as him, would not go down easy. Axmed was in serious pain but managed to get to his feet and ran down the alley. Horace looked up to see who saved him, it was Mozzy the bikie acquaintance from Denmark. Still in shock, Horace mumbled:

"Thanks lad, please call an Ambulance."

Mozzy was in two minds about chasing the big African but thought that police should have no problem finding him in a small place like Broome. He and Horace then ran back to Trevor where Boil was standing over the dying man holding Horace's bowler hat:

"Ambos and coppers on the way, but your mate is a goner."

Horace knelt beside Trevor, there was blood everywhere, with his last fading breath he said:

"Top pocket, leather pouch, can you see that Susan gets it in Sydney, tell her I lov..."

Horace took the leather pouch out, and held onto Trevor's hand, "I'll do my best", but the words were met with a last breath.

The bikers had arrived in Broome, as noisy as an aircraft, and Horace had no complaints it was great timing. The ambulance took Trevor's body to the coroner, and the police took details and description of the killer from the bikers. Horace was asked to go to the police station to give some more details about what he knew of the deceased, this took the best part of the night. He told them about Gladys Trussell and the Asians in Kojonup who were seeking Trevor's where abouts. He gave their description but had no other information. He didn't tell the police about the leather pouch. Horace had given a promise that he would deliver to someone who Trevor obviously loved and he would carry out that wish, when he eventually arrived back in Sydney.

Horace kept the anxiety caused by the event to himself. He was offered some counselling but refused. Time was the only cure that he needed, or so he thought. The Police set up roadblocks on the few roads out of Broome and conducted a full area search. An identikit picture was made and the airport was watched. The police now had enough information on this exotic animal export business. It was well financed internationally, and the murderer was probably shipped out immediately after the stabbing. They were puzzled by the mix of cultures in this case and aware that other agencies would now take note.

The following night Horace met up with Mozzy and Boil in the sportsman's bar and gave them a proper thank you, with a round of beers. They were nonchalant about it all, to them it was just another day on the road. Horace chatted for a while with the guys and heard Chilli Jam singing in the other bar, so he decided to try again to say hello to his old mate.

Horace had an interesting catch-up with Chilli, he knew all about the murder, the bikies and the funny fellow in the bowler hat.

"I figured that was you straight away Horace," he laughed.

Chilli had found himself a partner. Horace met Veronica and he thought they seemed suited. Together their lives were heading in a new direction which was pleasing. They were finishing up at the Roey that night and moving to the Cable Beach resort for a two-night gig.

"I'm going over there as well,' said Horace, 'and looking forward to that sunset camel ride and hopefully less drama."

The next day Horace packed up and was about to leave when a police officer showed up at the door. He had come around to see how he was, and to let him know that they notified Gladys about the sad death of her son Trevor. Horace asked if they had any details on Susan, but it turns out the Gladys didn't even know her maiden name. He thanked the officer and got Gladys's phone number, so he could ring to offer his condolences. He was thinking if he couldn't trace Susan, when he got back to Sydney, the least he could do was to send the leather pouch to her.

Cable Beach was only six kilometres away, and thankfully not on the Broome aviation flight path. On arrival Horace went to the bar for a drink, and to his surprise sitting at a table was Waiehu. The encounter was just what he needed to keep his subconscious anxiety over Trevor's murder in check. She was pleased to see him, they chatted and laughed for a while. He felt like confiding in her over the murder that was still on his mind but decided not to. He liked this lady and just needed some escape from the memory of it. They ended up talking for hours about their lives and interest, Horace even told her of his love of Shakespeare. They both agreed to book a sunset camel ride together. Waiehu then told him she had a surprise adventure that he may appreciate:

"Do you want to do some more time travelling Horace? Have you ever seen dinosaur footprints? Coupled with the contrasting colours of the land and exceptional bright blue water, we are in for a treat. There are 130-million-year-old Sauropod dinosaur footprints around Broome. They are recognised as the most significant in the world, and we're in luck, as there is a super low tide tomorrow, and that's the best time to see them."

Horace was excited at the prospect, once again this wonderful woman had captured his imagination, he was starting to feel a real attraction to this lady, despite the twelve years in age difference.

There was an extremely loud noise coming up the road from Broome, which got Horace's attention:

"It looks like the 'Great Australian Blight' tribe were spending a few nights here as well. This camel ride is going to be memorable, and exciting Waiehu; my forecast is for cloudless skies and noisy old guys."

Waiehu's plan to visit the dinosaur footprints was everything she said it would be, Horace was amazed. The next day they booked their sunset camel ride. They were on camels one and two in the line-up. It proceded down the beach just on sunset, it was a magical experience. As it turned out all their recent contacts were lined up behind them. There was Chilli and Veronica, they were followed by about eight ageing bikers, all whooping it up on an adventure down the sand on Cable Beach. It was a sunset to remember. That night they all sat around the bar at the resort exchanging stories. Horace was in his element; his notebook of experiences was filling fast. He had folded up the funeral suit and placed it at the bottom of his case. His Australian wardrobe was growing as well, he now wore his thongs on the beach and no longer called them flip-flops. Horace was amazed at the way some Australians interacted. The group of aging bikies, with funny names, now blended in laughter and mateship, with a Japanese Marine Biologist, a country rocker, and his new bird, plus a slightly rotund English gent who wore a bowler hat. Life was a wonder.

The next day Chilli and Veronica made their way to their next port of call the Halls Creek Hotel. After one night there, Chilli had a gig at Emma Gorge Resort in the El Questro Wilderness Park. They told Horace they planned to see the sights, including the Zebedee Springs permanent natural thermal waters and a bush walk and a swim in the crystal-clear pool under a waterfall. Once again Horace was amazed at what this country had on offer, within its vastness.

The bikers were also heading out, but they had a different destination. Mozzy told Horace they were heading to Derby and then to Halls Creek to meet up with a support vehicle. Boil jumped in with a brag.

"Yep, we're heading to Alice, and the Rock the hard way, via the Tanami Desert route, hence the support vehicle."

"That's a bold adventure for guys on bikes, isn't it?" asked Horace.

"We're not fools," said Mozzy, "we have a five-star four-wheel drive Mercedes truck support organised, carrying all the beer, food, camping gear and communication equipment we could possibly need, and then some."

"And you should see the two cute birds driving the rigg," laughed Boil.

"Well enjoy the adventure fellas, it sounds like fun, and thanks again for your help the other night."

With that the mighty roar of bikes ignited, and the 'Great Australian Blight' tribe, headed east, and beyond the flight path of another roar, which was just landing and rattling the windows in Broome.

Horace was shy, but also thinking about asking Waiehu to share a vehicle in the journey across the north to Darwin. He was feeling a lot closer with her, than he had a right to be. It turned out she suggested it first, which stunned him a bit. They stayed for another night at the resort, and over dinner under the stars, they both talked again about their backgrounds. Horace learnt about life in Fujiyama. Her parents loved Hawaii and named her Waiehu. She told him,

"It's Hawaiian meaning, was going the extra mile in the rough waters of life."

Waiehu learnt about Horace and his travel adventures, plus growing up in the Cotswolds. Horace laughed,

"My name is from the Latin Horatius, meaning time, and combined with my adventures and your knowledge, I'm now a time-traveller."

"Remember Horace," *'there are more things in heaven and earth, Horatio, than are dreamt of in your philosophy.'*

With that piece of Hamlet, Horace fell in love.

The next day Horace sent three postcards with sunset camel ride pictures. One went to Fiona in Silverwater prison, the others to his Mum and Beryl back in the Cotswolds, he didn't mention Waiehu to her. They handed in their hire cars at the airport and acquired a four-wheel drive with all the bells and whistles they would need. There was a bit of argy-bargy about drop off points and extra dollars, but *'Finding Earth Magazine'* will pick up the tab. As they waited for their car Waiehu told Horace of her plans:

"Sadly Horace, we will have to part ways in Darwin, I have contractual arrangements with Queensland

University and I must fly to Cairns and be on Lizard Island within two weeks. That said, how about this for an agenda; a visit to Derby, the gate way to Australia, if only the Government realised it. While there visit the giant Boab tree jail. Then a helicopter ride over the Bungle Bungle's National Park, and a boat ride on Lake Argyle at Kununurra. We could finish off with another boat adventure at Katherine Gorge on the way back to Darwin, knowing we have witnessed some of the best sites Australia has to offer."

Horace just smiled; all his English Christmases had come at once with this wonderful intelligent lady.

"Lead the way," he said, "but we will share the driving."

CHAPTER 9... A TOWN LIKE ALICE

(C... this is a Tanami Desert diversion, while Horace falls deeper in love)

Chilli dropped Veronica off at the Halls Creek hotel to check-in and drove to the general store for some drinks and nibbles. He parked the van and noticed people gathering around Halls Creek Civic Hall, he could hear music. A local Yolngu Aborigine group called 'The Flakes' were strumming away with some cool sounds. There was a gold coin sign at the entry to the centre, Chilli grabbed one from the consul and headed to the music.

The support vehicle, which was going to assist the *'Great Australian Blight'* tribe across the Tanami Desert was awaiting their arrival in Halls Creek. It was operated by two sisters, Anne and Gayle Bagnall. Boil was in luck; they were both single and stunners. Gayle also heard the music and headed for the entry. She gave the attendant a ten-dollar note and she received four two-dollar coins in change.

(C...time to move on, Veronica had spent it wisely.)

Gayle noticed the coin's message as she hopped in the van,

"Hey, Anne check this out, *'love is a currency spend it wisely.'* Do you think karma is about to take over my will?"

"No, but it may be an omen to be wary"

* * *

It was a four-day trek across the corrugated Tanami Desert and the aging bikies felt every bump, as did the coin in the Mercedes truck consul. Boil hit on Anne at every camp out. When he had no luck with her, he tried Gayle, to no avail. Still, the beer was cold from the truck fridge and the open expanse of the Milky Way through the clear night skies made even the toughest bikie think about their place in the scheme of things. Gayle feigned interest and did ask Boil how he got his name; his response was:

"No one could spell carbuncle."

That painful episode in Boil's life always had the group in stiches of laughter. When terrible things happen, they always seem to involve Boil. On an earlier ride around Tasmania, a small pimple on his bum began to grow. It quadrupled in size after three days on the road, and he had to ride standing up until they found a doctor. They found one in Queenstown who lanced and dressed it. After that they called him Boil, funny thing his real name was Lance Carbone.

The 'Great Australian Blight' tribe, and the support vehicle ladies, spent the last night of their epic journey across the Tanami Desert at the turn off to the Laramba Aboriginal Settlement. They were still two hundred kilometres from Alice Springs. The next day's drive would be a short one, so this was their last night with the girls. It was to be a party night, and a thank you to the lovely lady escorts for their assistance on the trek. Gayle and Anne were not going to Alice, their plan was to turn left at the

Stuart Highway and head to Katherine. Boil still had an eye for Gayle and she was a lot friendlier now. Although the bikers were all tired and weary after the bumpy ride, they still managed to finish off most of the food and grog left in the support vehicle.

Once again, the night sky was ablaze with stars. It was cool and still. Boil was still hoping for more, he sat with Gayle chatting about their lives for about an hour. He realised that a relationship with this lady was just a dream for the moment and would need further work. Gayle gave him her contact details, as she thought about the coin's message, *'love is a currency spend it wisely.'* Boil was trying to be cool about it all, he had drunk only a few beers and decided to retire a little bit earlier than the rest of the blokes, he was a little sad. He told Gayle he was going to sleep out in the open that night, he was thinking that she might change her mind. He rolled out his swag and bag near a rocky outcrop adjacent to the campsite, looked up at the vast array of stars and felt tiny, he quickly dozed off thinking about Gayle.

Boil woke early, he was watching a magic sunrise in the east, as it spread its warming rays out over the vast flat red land. As he laid on his swag he noticed a movement to his left, it was a tiny wiggling blackworm pointing skyward, adjacent to a boulder. He reached out to touch it. One of the most venomous land snakes in the world is the desert death adder and the Tanami Desert is a perfect home. Their first line of defence against predators is to not be detected in the first place. They remain still and blend in with the terrain. When hunting, they wiggle their worm-like tail to lure prey, and the lure is always near their flattened head. They strike lightning fast, too fast for a yawning bikie.

The silent death adder struck without warning and latched onto his hand, then just as quick took off between two rocks. His scream woke the camp and Mozzy and Gayle came running over. With luck, Gayle was a wealth of knowledge, she quickly immobilised his arm and wrapped it with a bandage from the shoulder to the bite. Symptoms, when bitten, range from paralysis to abdominal pain, headaches, and drowsiness, then death. Dry bites are common with death adders, they don't like to waste their venom, so sometimes antivenom is not required.

"What did it look like?" she asked Boil.

"It was about two foot long with a flathead and a tiny black tail."

"That's a desert death adder, we must get you to a medical clinic and fast."

Gayle was now trying to ease Boils blood pumping anxiety:

"With a bit of luck, you will be ok mate, most of these are dry bites, and without venom."

Despite its remote location the Tanami Desert Road has Indigenous Communities. Yuendumu is four hours northwest of Alice Springs and is one of the largest Aboriginal communities in central Australia. Another is Laramba, which is two hours closer, but of no help to Boil because both the medical centres would be shut at that hour, and there was a good chance that they didn't have the antivenom.

They tried ringing the health clinic at Laramba, with no luck. Alice Springs was their only choice. Some of the group relayed Boil's bike to the Laramba settlement and stayed there. The rest followed the van to Alice. Boil was starting to show some effects of the bite, he was a bit hot and clammy, but laughed it off as been too close to nurse Gayle. Boil's luck was running out, by the time they reached the turn off to Stuart Highway he had a raging headache and abdominal pains. They were ten minutes out from Alice, when they saw the road train approaching.

The gigantic road trains on the Stuart Highway are more commonly known as triple bogies. They approach the unwary driver, coming from the other direction at thundering speeds. It's only a two-lane highway, in the middle of nowhere, when you see it coming, and think what to do? Seconds later it's on you. The shock wave hits and displaces the air, the car drifts onto the gravel on the shoulder, you don't have a choice. It is a frightening and crazy moment where you swim through a cloud of gravel and dust, until the car stops. Once the carnage is over you sit there for a moment, then expletives flow at the departing truck. You then inspect for damage and hopefully you can continue the journey. This wasn't the case for the ladies and Boil in the van, a pothole on the shoulder flipped them like a coin.

(C...and one coin, (me), landed on the opposite side of the road, just as another car stopped to help)

❋ ❋ ❋

Doug and Layla Pitt had just left Alice Springs after a wonderful five days of sightseeing. They had walked around Uluru and watched it change colours at sunrise and sunset. Then they hiked the Martian landscape around the conglomerate mounds of Kata Tjuta. From the Kings Canyon rim walk, they drove down the back road along the world's oldest river the Finke. Then on to the Hermannsburg Mission and the acoustic Church. In Alice Springs they visited the fabulous Desert Park and the old Telegraph station. For a nurse from a country village call Borenore, it was the experience of a lifetime, and both Layla and Doug were on a high. They had just started their journey to Darwin when they witnessed the accident.

As Doug pulled up, he rang for an ambulance, Layla ran across the road and helped get the people out, the van was a right-off, but everybody was just shaken and not injured. Gayle told Layla about Boil. They walked him clear, kept him still and waited. Mozzy, said he would take him on the bike but Boil was now in no shape to be a pillion passenger. They heard the siren in the distance and it arrived minutes later. They rushed Boil to Alice Springs base hospital just in time to administer the antivenom. Gayle and Anne went with him.

Mozzy thanked Layla and Doug for their help. As they got back in their car, Layla picked up a gold coin adjacent to the door.

"Check this out Doug, it's got a message on it, *'love is a currency spend it wisely,'* isn't that the truth."

Boil's carbuncle days of bad luck were now behind him, he survived. Because the girls had to await a replacement vehicle, Boil got a chance to go on a date with Gayle. Things were looking up, she now called him Lance. The *'Great Australian Blight'* tribe had regrouped in Alice Springs, they were now on their way to the Rock, Oodnadatta, and the Nullarbor to complete their journey. The *'Grim Reaper'* was still many miles, and years away.

* * *

Doug Pitt had no siblings, he was a big tough guy, and in dog terms, you could say he was a real mongrel. This was not casting dispersions on his character, but more about the roots of his ancestry. His grandparents were Scottish and Indian, but his parents were more worldly. Doug's mother was born in Canada, his father was born in France and Doug was born in Iran. He was only three when the family had to migrate to Australia for security. The Shar had been overthrown and the Ayatollah took over.

Currently, Doug was a miner, it was a tough industry and he had grown into a *'Jack of all trades'*, his nickname was Digger. He had worked all over Australia and was in his forties when he first met his wife Layla in Orange. Layla was a nurse from a country village call Borenore, west of Orange. She loved it there because it was one of those little places with a population of no more than four hundred people, but she felt a need to explore the country. They had been living in Broken Hill for a year when he received a job offer in Cairns. They decided to have a driving holiday from Alice Springs to Darwin and then head east to start his next appointment.

CHAPTER 10...TOP END EVOLUTION

Horace and Waiehu arrived in Darwin all hot and sweaty. Waiehu made herself comfortable at a motel, while Horace, still dressed for the heat, as per normal the first place he made for was a pub. On the way he passed a hairdresser and decided to have a number two, to help with the humidity. It was one of those old fashion places with the red and white post, it was called Antonio's Cuts. Horace sat down but was immediately directed to the leather operating chair by a large man with a thick imperial moustache. Horace thought he looked a bit like Joseph Stalin. It was Antonio, he wasn't Italian or Russian, just an old Aussie with a wealth of local knowledge, whose name was Tony Barber. Horace just accepted the fact that surnames dictated careers. Tony did an excellent job, and even trimmed those other facial hairy places where hair seems to grow better than on your head. As he trimmed, Tony gave Horace a quick history of Darwin and places to drink. He left feeling cooler and wiser.

Horace loved old pubs, they reminded him of home, sadly Australia didn't have many. According to Tony Barber, two Darwin pubs survived three cyclones and the war. Sadly, the 'Victoria Hotel' finally shut shop in 2014, through debt, not bombs or cyclones. In a typical Australian fashion, more damage was caused to this hotel by a soldier's riot in September 1941 than the Japanese bombing raids. The other pub was Hotel Darwin, known as the *'Grand Old Duchess'*, it stood for sixty-three years. It was finally demolished in 1999, then rebuilt. Both hotels survived Darwin's Cyclone Tracey, the mother of all storms. It hit on Christmas Day 1974 and killed seventy-one people. That left Horace with only one choice for a beer, Hotel Darwin, a shadow of its former glory. He walked in and the first person he saw was a real estate agent, not a funeral director. He sat at one end of a large table in the lounge area. At the other end was a bloke he didn't recognize, he was a miner named Doug Pitt.

Doug and Horace struck up a conversation about outback travel. Horace nearlly laughed when he heard Doug's last name, but he controlled himself, knowing now how right he was when it came to Australian names and careers. There was a slight twist in his names assessment in this pub however, the publicans name was Steven Drinkwater.

"You can call me Digger, everybody else does. My parents had a great sense of humour."

Horace just smiled and relayed his thoughts on names and career choices.

Doug, then spoke of Alice Springs, Uluru, and Kings Canyon:

"That rock was spectacular; do you know it's just hardened clay washed up from an ancient river."

"No, I didn't" said Horace, "I had the quicky tourist trek to the Red Centre about ten years ago, it was dry and dusty. I was in and out so fast I didn't need a fan, but I had to take my coat and tie off and roll my sleeves up. I remember the heat, the flies, the red rock, and a visit to a desert park where every step you took crunched under your feet. I also saw a Sturt Pea, a Thorny Devil lizard that looked like a demon and a spider the size of a mouse that barked like a dog."

"That's called a Barking Spider," said Doug, "that Desert Park was pretty special, my wife loved it, you will meet her in a moment, she is in the gaming room, Layla loves to have a flutter occasionally."

Horace had no idea what a flutter was, he assumed it was some sort of machine, but politely continued:

"You certainly see and hear some strange things out here. I was near the border with the Northern Territory and an old German guy named Klaus was on the side of the road. He was watering his camel. This scrawny beast of burden was towing an old half-truck with solar power panels on the top, it was Klaus's mobile home. He walked the road with the camel, with no destination in mind, a toothless warrior of the outback. He spoke in broken English and smelt like he had been walking with camels for his entire life. He wanted to swap my bowler hat for his well-worn Akubra. When I say worn, it's not an exaggeration, it was a thing of abstract beauty, sweat plastered, camel dung, crocodile teeth marks, and if you placed it on the ground it would run away on the legs of tiny life forms. I said no thanks. Such are the characters you meet in the Australian outback."

"That's spot-on Horace, on our journey here we helped at an accident, just north of Alice Springs. A road train truck caused a van to roll. There was a group of bikers and some girls in the van, they were incredibly lucky no one was injured, but one bloke called Boil, who was in the van was in dire straits he had been bitten by a deadly snake. They had to rush him to Alice Springs."

"Now, that's a coincidence I met Boil, and that bike

group twice. First time was near Albany and they saved me from a stabbing in Broome, they are great blokes. I even went on a camel ride with them."

"Wow! I heard about that bloke dying in Broome, on the radio, you certainly get around Horace, you should write a book."

"I'm a travel writer for *'Finding Earth Magazine'*, they pay me for the fun."

Quoting Shakespeare again, he followed up with:

'All the world's a stage, and all the men and women are merely players.'

Layla came up to the table looking glum.

"This is Horace," said Doug, "he is a travel writer."

"How did you go with the flutter machines?" said Horace.

Doug laughed, "My wife calls me Digger, so from now on Horace, I'm calling her Flutter."

Layla picked up on the banter, OK she said:

"You should never flutter with pokies in pubs; they just soak up your money. I spent twenty dollars and all my coins, and in all that time I got two drops."

Horace now learnt that flutter was a verb.

"Australia seems to have a lot of clubs; do they all have these pokies?"

"More than our fair share," said Doug as he turned to his wife and laughed:

"You lost twenty bucks? Get thee to a nunnery." With that Horace laughed as well,

"I thought I was the only Shakespeare mimic in town, now there are two of us."

"No mate, mine is but High School Hamlet."

They had a few more drinks, shared some more stories and Horace said he may run into them again in Cairns. He then grabbed his bowler hat and took his leave to go back to the motel, his admiration of Australian characters was growing daily.

As they were leaving the pub an hour later, Layla turned to Doug with that glum look again and laughed:

"You won't believe it Digger, I accidently put that special coin in the *'one arm bandit'*, damn, I didn't spend it wisely, did I?"

* * *

Horace was now planning on taking Waiehu to a fancy restaurant if he could find one. On arrival into Darwin, he had noticed a few real estate agent's images and only one funeral director poster. As he walked to the motel luck showed its hand, he spotted the two real estate agents. He jumped at the opportunity to ask these gents the name of the best restaurant in Darwin. They both pointed to the marina.

Horace's estate agents knew their way around Darwin restaurants. The Oyster Bar at the marina was just the treat for a travel writer and a marine biologist. The night's conversation was all about crustations, molluscs and fish, as they devoured the best of the cuisine on offer. They also talked about Australian gambling habits, and what would lead people to race cane toads. Afterwards they walked back to the motel and stopped on the way for a drink at the *'Grand Old Duchess,'* so Waiehu could try fluttering a poker machine for the first time in her life. She played a two-dollar machine with an outlay of ten dollars and quickly got bored. Horace just watched on. She was down to her last bet and the machine had its first pay out, it was ten dollars, so she cashed it in and received a hand full of coins for her effort.

"Well, that was a waste of time." She smiled at Horace and put the coins in her purse. They then went for a night cap coffee. She would not discover the special engraved coin until she was on the plane to Cairns. Horace was feeling closer to Waiehu and he finally confided in her over Trevor's murder. She showed him true concern and said that it was good to talk about upsetting events in life. He took her advice on board and thanked her. He was now thinking about taking the relationship to the next level that night, but he was unsure of Japanese mating rituals. Time was running out, Waiehu was flying out the next day. She had a sensual smile on her face when Horace escorted her to the door of her room, but all he received was a kiss on the cheek, her phone number and email address. Horace was not into Facebook or Twitter; he just asked her to give him a call when she was safe and settled on Lizard Island. He was wise and pragmatic enough to let nature take its course, but in his heart, he now knew he wanted more.

They dropped the vehicle off at the airport the next day, had a hug and said their farewells. Horace was taking a cab back to Darwin where, in the following week, he had a Litchfield and Kakadu tour organised. He waited till the plane took off, his mind was no longer on funeral directors or real estate agents, just a cute and intelligent marine biologist.

On the plane, Waiehu checked her purse to pay for a bottle of water and noticed an inscription on one of the coins:

"Love is a currency spend it wisely, ha! work and life choices never seem to synchronise."

Waiehu smiled, her mind was now on fluttering poker machines, cane toads, and a man who wore a Derby bowler hat. She now knew she wanted him in her life.

When Waiehu landed at Cairns she could hear a beautiful tune being played by a Flautist somewhere near the exit gates. She retrieved her bags and made her way to the sound. A beautiful young lady dressed in a purple robe was busking for gold coins. The tune was haunting and inviting. Without giving it a thought Waiehu deposited some coins into the cup. The woman's smile was enchanting. She had a name tag on that said, *'Penelope a weaver of charm'*. It was only later when Waiehu was checking into the motel that she realised, she had given the special coin away.

The next day was a quiet one for Horace, he was feeling a little lonely. He had been on the road now for nearly three months. Although his mind was lapping up the experiences, his body was starting to tire, he needed a few days of self-time and to catch up on his notes. The *'Finding Earth Magazine'* boss had called for an update and said he looked forward to catching up in London in a few months. This made Horace think once again about Waiehu, but he locked that away in a special part of his brain for a while. His self-time lasted just one day, after which his battery was recharged for more encounters.

It was a steamy and muggy Darwin morning, just weeks before the start of the wet season. Horace was now looking forward to the next two days of bus tours. He was dressed in shorts and a tee-shirt, trying to look and feel cool. The logo on the shirt front summed up his mood, it read:

'So, this is Darwin what did you expect?' The rear of the shirt contained the warning; *'Our sea has life-forms that are protected from swimmers, enter at your own risk.'*

He toured the Darwin War Museum and walked the foreshore where the one sided *'Battle of Darwin'* took place. For obvious reasons he didn't go for a swim, nor did he smile at a crocodile. He went to the shops for some new clothes and then found himself back at the *'Grand Old Duchess'*. The first person he recognised and had a chat with was a funeral director, whose name was Iain Grieves, which didn't surprise Horace in the least.

Iain was an interesting character. He told Horace all about Darwin's death statistics. Alcohol not crocodiles killed most people. Morbid curiosity let the conversation continue for a few minutes. Horace's input to the talk of death, was that William Shakespeare in 1747 placed a curse on the grave robbers in Stratford-upon-Avon, that they would be haunted if they touched his bones.

After that Horace changed the subject:

"You live in an amazing place Iain, it may be full of deserts and crowded coastal cities, but in Australia the scenery and landscapes are pure art and sculptured wonders. There are so many highlights, if I had to pick one of the best, it was the helicopter flight over the Bungle Bungles."

"Yes, I have heard that they are spectacular Horace. One day my wife and I will get there."

"There were no doors on the helicopter, it was a thrill. My lady traveling companion held me close, she was fearful that she might fall out. We looked down at these conglomerate domes, time traveling along ancient riverbeds. There were people walking the trails, one day I will return and do that myself."

Horace stopped talking for a moment, he was thinking about Waiehu holding him close and laughing with fear. It was that moment of contact when he fell in love. He continued talking about the cruise at Katherine Gorge and the Angler fish spitting at people's shiny objects from the water's surface, but his thoughts were now elsewhere. The bus was due at 8am the following morning, so he was not about to have a big session with Iain. He said his goodnights and wished him success. Only later thinking, that success for Iain meant more people dying.

The bus tour to Litchfield arrived right on time. It was full of spritely senior citizens who chatted on and on about their medical conditions and their prearranged funeral plans with Mr Grieves, Horace's former drinking companion. The two-metre-tall magnetic termite mounds stopped the chatter for a few minutes, while the tour guide explained how termites could build without a compass. It turned out to be a wonderful day, all the aging Mary and Margaret widows had their good eye on young Horace. He was the only one who went for a swim at the Wangi Falls and the only one to get sunburnt. One of the more explicit Mary's made a comment, with a snigger:

"Unaccustomed Poms will always fall prey to our burning sun God Ra."

To the smart sun blocked senior lustful ladies, Horace in his budgie smugglers, looked like *'Jungle Jim'*, the Johnny Weissmuller of Wangi, braving the sun and the possibility of crocodiles, to swim under the falls.

While the senior ladies were busy chatting, the tour guide mentioned the Styrofoam balls floating in the water hole. They were there to indicate the presence of crocs. The crocs love to bite the balls, hence no bite marks, no crocs. Horace took this on notice as Aussie bull-shite and bravely took the plunge, but not before checking the balls. It seems some of the ladies overheard the tour guide, but they still admired his bravery, because one of them read a sign, *'new styro-balls fitted this morning'*. They didn't tell Horace.

Horace had checked out of his Darwin motel after one last night of liver destruction, with his newly found real-estate mates. The tourist season in Darwin was normally April to November. Horace was in luck; he had booked the last short tour before the wet season. The forecasters also said the rains would be late this year. The bus he organised had a boat tour and some short view stops on the way to Kakadu, and all up it would be a four-hour journey, with lunch provided. He had pre-arranged the Kakadu visit as a one-way trip and would organise his own transport for the return journey to Darwin. Kakadu National Park is Australia's largest and Horace had three things in mind for his visit there. He wanted to witness the rock art creation stories, find out about Aboriginal first contact with Europeans in the territory, and he was really looking forward to a flight over Arnhem land. He had phoned ahead to book the hotel and the flight. The plane would fly over the Ranger uranium mines and other wonders on the Arnhem land plateau.

In 1820, explorer Phillip King didn't know the difference between an alligator and a crocodile. He named a river he found, on his journey across the top end, the Alligator River. He reported that you could walk across the river on the backs of these five-metre beast, there were so many of them. On the way to Jabiru the bus stopped on the Arnhem highway, at the bridge over the very same Alligator River. They were heading to the 'Yellow Water' billabong, on the Kakadu Highway for a pre-arranged boat tour. Horace was thinking about crocodiles and foam balls when the bus driver announced:

"A Jabiru is a stork like bird with long red legs, and there's one over there to your left, beside the river."

Horace was glad he wasn't on the boat yet, or it would have capsized, with bus passengers all leaning to the left at once. He had noticed on bus journeys in the past that instant glances on natural wonders was all that could be expected with time schedules. He remarked to some of the passengers that getting out of the bus to look at a Jabiru on the riverbank full of five metre man-eating reptiles from the age of the dinosaurs was not a clever idea. They all agreed.

The bus went through the township of Jabiru and finally arrived at the 'Yellow Waters' billabong; the bird life was amazing. They even got to see a jabiru and a crocodile up close, from the perceived safety of the boat, and it didn't capsize. Horace was in awe of Kakadu's changing landscapes and vivid colours. The journey continued to the Crocodile Hotel, called Gagudju. It was built to look like a giant crocodile from the air but had the symmetry of a Lego creation. The highlight of Horace's stay in Kakadu was to be a flight over Arnhem land, but sadly this time there would be no Waiehu to hold close and share the experience with.

❉ ❉ ❉

While Horace was counting crocodiles in the Alligator River, the Americans that he met in Walpole, Shane and Clarissa Huckster, were on the Great Ocean Road in Victoria. They were looking at what was left of the fast eroding Twelve Apostles and heading for a night in Apollo Bay, when they received a call from Tebogo Modise. The call was short and direct on a burner phone, they would now have to get rid of.

"Change of plans you will be flying home via Brisbane." He then hung up.

The Hucksters were cool criminals, change did not faze them.

"What was that about Shane?"

"Must be some issues in Sydney, its great news, we get to see some more of the East Coast, we will be flying out of Brisbane."

"I bet that coast is not as spectacular as this one"

"No, just different darling."

They stopped at the next secluded view spot for a selfie photo, there were no other cars about. The burner phone was discarded over the edge. As it sank into the clear blue and foamy Great Southern Ocean at Gibson Beach, Clarissa asked:

"Where are we heading next Shane?"

"I was thinking the inland route via the Sovereign Hill historic village at Ballarat then the back roads of country hospitality, all the way to Brisbane. There's no hurry honey, we are just tourists having fun."

CHAPTER 11...THE AKUBRA FLIGHT

Horace was checking into the hotel when he noticed an entertainment sign. It was on a trestle adjacent to a large glass enclosure that contained a realistic underwater view of a crocodile chasing a barramundi fish. Horace thought about the barramundi he had seen at Katherine Gorge, there were several swimming in circles under the spitting angler fish. When he stopped thinking about food chains, his focus on the sign took over. The group performing that night were called *'The Sultana Bran Flakes'*, he immediately thought of Chilli-Jam Johnson. A moment later Veronica walked past him, heading for the pool.

"Hi Veronica, don't you get around!"

"G'day Horace, it's a long story, we have a new band."

"I'll drop off my bags and meet you at the pool in five."

When Horace went back to the pool, Chilli was there with three Aboriginal chaps. After introductions, he found out that the group were a local country-rock group called the *'Flakes'*. They all hit it off at Halls Creek and decided to form a new band. Chilli had a huge smile on his face:

"What are you doing here old mate, and it looks like you have swapped the bowler hat for some budgie smugglers?"

"The hats in the room, and the togs, that's what

we gentlemen call them, are to cool off in that pool." He laughed, "and I'm here to see crocodiles and have a flight over Arnhem Land as well."

"Guess what Horace, we now call ourselves the 'Sultana Bran Flakes', catchy eh?"

"What sort of music do you play?"

"It's a mixture of my soulful ballads and Aboriginal rock, didgeridoos, and all. It's our first gig tonight. The boys are all from the local Yolngu people, we have been practising all week. Their uncle is a bigwig with the land council here and got us the start. I'll introduce you tonight. His name is Gurigal Cudgegol, a real character, he flies for Oenpelli Air and calls himself Plane Bob. He will most likely be your pilot, good luck!" he laughed.

Horace walked into the lounge area that night to the sound of a haunting didgeridoo followed by soft guitar and drums. The words in the song were about a cowboy's harmonica, enchanting Veronica by a billabong in the gulf country alongside a bush called Japonica. It all seemed to work, the audience clapped and the next song, a Slim Dusty classic had them smooching on the dance floor.

During the break Horace met Plane Bob, he was more hair than face, but his white toothy smile made people around him feel comfortable. He was tall and lean and had a regal look about him. They talked about the top-end and its history. He told Horace that the Japonica bush in the song was from a local legend, where in a pre-European visit by the Chinese, they gifted the locals with the plant. It was said that the Loquat fruit from that plant had special medicinal properties when it was consumed as a tea. The music started up again and Bob jumped up and departed saying:

"See you in the morning at nine, my English friend, I'm your pilot so don't be late."

As Horace watched him walk away with the large strides of a man on a mission, he couldn't help but think of the Aboriginal on the Australian two-dollar coin that he had read about. The engraving was of Gwoya Jungarai, a survivor of an Aboriginal massacre. The artful image was of a tall and lean man standing proud beneath the Southern Cross, with a long flowing beard and a powerful chest crossed with tribal scars:

'And this is my pilot?'

The next day after breakfast, Horace met the Oenpelli Air bus out the front of the hotel. The bus driver was Plane Bob, the versatile pilot, and Horace was the only customer for the day. He had folded his funeral director's suit into the bottom of his suitcase and put his bowler hat into a box. The heat and humidity had now temporarily altered his fashion sense. He had also purchased a new outfit in Darwin. He was now the aging Steve Irwin look-a-like, complete with Khaki safari shirt and shorts and a flash Akubra hat. Bob just looked him up and down, and with a smirk said:

"Let me guess, Crocodile Dundee's Sunday best."

Horace just laughed, "at least I took the tags off."

That broke the ice, and Bob explained Horace's duty as the temporary co-pilot:

"Don't touch anything unless I scream eject. There is also some storm activity in the north, but we should be back before you get that new clobber wet. The proper wet season is still weeks away, I think"

Horace was starting to appreciate Plane Bobs humour.

The plane they would be in was not the normal unit, when there was only one customer the smaller single prop Cessna was used. 'It was old but air worthy,' said Bob. Horace saw some exposed wiring and seat damage, he was thinking about a Biggles adventure, but his excitement dulled any fear.

Bob was a proud local and spoke about his country:

"Arnhem Land is around 500 km from Darwin Horace and covers an area bigger than Ireland. It is close to 100 thousand square kilometres and is one of the largest Aboriginal owned reserves in Australia. It is perhaps best known for its isolation, beauty, rock art, and music. You won't guess Horace, but about 16,000 people live here and 12,000 of them are Aboriginal Yolngu people. We call our country Djulpan and we are the traditional owners of all the land here."

The first view was of the Ranger uranium mines. Bob was a wealth of knowledge on yellow cake mining as it was called and the Jabiluka controversy further north. They flew south over the spectacular Jim Jim Falls and Twin Falls, then headed across the Plateau to West Arnhem. Horace's view was now of ancient rivers meandering like giant snakes across an ochre-coloured landscape, with rocky time sculptured outcrops blending in with emerald coloured scrub and green palm trees. Bob explained how the Yolngu traversed the land by following song lines that carried messages in the chants, which gave them directions for food and water during the dry season.

They were about a half an hour into the flight when

Horace noticed Bob tapping the oil pressure gauge.

"Anything there to worry about Bob?"

"No sweat mate, it's just a dicky gauge, but get ready with that eject button."

The words no sweat and eject button rang the Biggles alarm bells in the Englishman's brain. He tightened his seatbelt, looked around the cabin for an eject button and a parachute, then took a death grip on the door handle. Plane Bob noticed the change in Horace's comfort zone and assured him all was well, after all they were insured. That's when everything went quiet:

"Houston, we have a problem, these things fly better with a working motor."

Bobs calmness was no longer working on Horace, his sun burnt face faded, he went white and broke out in a cold sweat. He looked wide eyed at Bob who was casually fiddling with knobs. The plane wasn't worried either, it just floated there like a glider. Horace apart from the fear, was thinking three things, gravity, Waiehu, and strangely at that moment Trevor's stabbing murder. That's when the motor noise started again.

"Well, the good news is the fuel blockage cleared and we don't have to make a river landing, those bloody crocs would give us hell, but we will have to make a slight diversion to Oenpelli air strip near Gunbalanya. Aunty Jill may have to put us up for the night while our capable mechanic Joe, flushes the plumbing and looks at the engine to see if the mice are on strike again."

"So, we are not going to die Bob?"

"No, she'll be wright mate, we won't charge you for the extra excitement on the flight and you'll love Aunty Jill. She works for the Injalak art company and that means you will get a free tour up Injalak Hill to see some very special rock art at the company's expense. But you will have to share a bed with her six children."

He laughed again, but seemed totally in control of the situation, this eased Horace's tension just a little.

"Just joking about the kids' mate, I'll radio ahead, they will have transport arranged to take us to Gunbalanya, and the good news is that the rain is holding off."

"Do they have a laundry and pub on site Bob? I may need a change of undies and a calming agent."

"Aunty will wash-em for you mate, and there's no pub, it's a dry town, but I do have my private stock of selective refreshments."

The landing was bumpy and dusty, but they got there with no need for the missing parachutes. As Horace jumped out of the plane, an out back willy-willy took his Akubra for a trip, it landed at the feet of Capable Joe, another amusing alias. He was the dead ringer of Plane Bob in size, but his hair was in a ponytail and he had no beard. It turned out they were twins; his real name was Mugaroi:

"G'day Horace I'm Joe, I bet that was an exciting trip mate. Bob loves that old plane I keep telling him, we should trade it in, but anyhow, welcome to Oenpelli."

Horace just smiled, he was starting to appreciate the cultural significance of Aboriginal humour and expressions. Only communication over vast periods of time could create such an eloquent language. Here he was standing with two Aboriginal men, with ancestry in this vast land, going back possibly more than sixty thousand years. They were Gurigal and Mugaroi Cudgegol, of the

Yolngu people from Gunbalanya on the Djulpan Plateau, flying planes out of Oenpelli.

'*Aesthetically sculptured by time,*' thought Horace, with his inbuilt thesaurus.

Aunty Jill epitomised the outback matriarch, she was a pearl in the oyster of struggle. Solving strife, offering wisdom, and soothing pain. She was cook, cleaner, talker, friend, guide, and mother to all, and she knew her culture. After washing his undies, she took Horace for a walk up Injalak Hill to see some very special rock art, and explained their ancient messages. Later that day she sold him a piece of local art. The picture detailed a dreamtime serpent carving the local rocky canyons. She told Horace how Yolngu art was spiritually connected to all local living things:

"The colours, dots, lines, and circles are from nature Horace. You just have to look at our local butterflies, like our swallowtails and lacewing to see the inspiration that has flowed in our culture for thousands of years. Art followed the song-lines and was shared by all. Go to Alice Springs and see the Yeperenye caterpillar with its colourful pixelated body, our art is nature, as are we."

That night after the tour with Aunty Jill, Plane Bob invited Horace to a special smoking ceremony and bush tucker dinner. Two of the younger boys from the tribe went with them to a secret camp site. They had painted their faces with white ceremonial stripes and then placed two on Horace's cheeks.

He was now thinking, '*I hope this event didn't involve any bleeding scar ceremonies.*'

Bob seemed to pick up on Horace's thoughts:

"Don't worry my English friend we will not initiate

you tonight with anything that involves blood, other than an occasional mosquito," he laughed.

Bob explained that women weren't allowed at this special men's only site, because they went there to be washed clean from any bad warrior spirits:

"If you have anything other than that plane flight fright to be rid of, Horace, tonight we will cleanse the evil spirits from you."

Horace immediately thought about Trevor Trussells gruesome death:

"Thank you Gurigal Cudgegol."

Plane Bob took that response as a sign of true respect. Few people could recall his name.

The boys were carrying some containers and stopping every now and then to dig up some yams and gather grubs with their knives from under tree bark. They also gathered some 'Billy Goat' plums and large Lilly pad leaves, telling Horace he was in for a treat. He was starting to feel a bit squeamish that his dinner was being harvested as he walked. He thought the yams were like potatoes, but he knew that the grubs were Aboriginal food. Plane Bob was silent and focused. Bob had been a stockman in his youth and was an old swagman when it came to cuisine. He was also adept at Aboriginal bush tucker. They arrived at a very secluded place near a Billabong and set about lighting a fire. As the fire grew Plane Bob and the boys started chanting a song in their native tongue.

Bob had a large piece of bark and scraped some of the fire onto it. He then placed some green shrub onto it and continued to chant. As the smoke began to rise, he beckoned Horace to wave his hands and swim through the smoke. Horace did so and was intrigued and felt very special.

"The smoke will wash away evil spirits Horace, to help you become one with nature. We are all part of the whole creation and all things are brothers and sisters to us, and you are now a brother with us."

Horace coughed and sneezed but thought of Trevor and other things that bothered him. He sat for ten minutes after the ceremony by the warmth of the fire, and strangely felt anxiety free for the first time in his life. He once again thanked Bob for the experience.

"It's time to eat Horace." Plane Bob was back in his stockman persona. "Have you ever seen a Murrumbidgee roll or had a damper and a cup of Billy tea?"

"No, I can't say I have."

"Well, for the damper we just need some flour and water, some special local bush tucker additives and some big green leaves. The tea is made by boiling water in a billy can, that's a tin can with a wire handle. Then we add some tea leaves, and then the secret men's business begins. We swing the billy over our head to settle the leaves. The swinging part is called a Murrumbidgee roll. Did you know the first product placement ever in an Australian song was in Banjo Paterson's *'Waltzing Matilda'*? There were two versions of that song Horace, the second version was added to help sell tea, and contained the chorus:

'He sang as he watched and waited 'til his Billy boiled.'

In the early 1900s a tea merchant with the Billy Tea company, secured permission to use the poem. And here we are, by a Billabong with a Billy of tea, but no Coolabah tree." Laughed Bob.

Once again, Plane Bob's bush knowledge amazed Horace. He was watching the preparation of the damper in the fire and all the gathered food stuff being placed onto Lilly leaves, when he noticed that some of the grubs were still moving. Bob had two billies on the fire, he finished the Murrumbidgee roll, poured the tea, broke open the steaming damper and said:

"Lads' dinner is served, hoe in!"

Bob grabbed the other billy from the fire and noticed the reluctance on Horace's face as he reached for the moving cuisine.

"You're welcome to try that if you like Horace, its good grub, but this billy has Aunty Jill's special lamb stew in it, if you prefer, it goes down well with the damper. It's always good to have a jumbuck in your tucker bag"

Plane Bob had a chuckle, and Horace a smirk of relief. He was now reciting *'Waltzing Matilda'* in his mind, and decided he really liked this bloke. After the dinner they walked back to Aunty Jills, had a couple of beers and then they all hit the sack, and with luck Horace had the bed to himself.

Horace left Gunbalanya with a new understanding of the Australian Aboriginal. He thanked Aunty Jill for her help and knowledge. Capable Joe had patched up the Cessna, back to a modest working order, but a major service would be needed in Darwin. Plane Bob was keen to get back to Jabiru, he had a full tour organised in the larger plane. He told Horace if he stayed just one more day in the hotel, he would fly him back to Darwin for free.

'Next stop was Cairns,' he thought, *'and hopefully a catch up with Waiehu for Christmas.'*

Horace had a new admiration of Bob's flying skill,

and even without a parachute, this offer was better than a bus full of senior medical complaints. This also offered a chance to have one more night of melancholy tunes with the 'The Sultana Bran Flakes', and a few draft beers with Plane Bob.

The flight back to Darwin was not without tight hand grips and nonchalant humour. The view from the co-pilot's portal was of black storm clouds and lightning strikes on the horizon. To this Bob's comment on the wet season changed:

"Well, I hate to admit it, but I was wrong, the wet season is here, and it's going to be a big one. My guess, La Nina is back in town and we may have to start naming cyclones by numbers. Your stay in Cairns may be a damp one old mate."

CHAPTER 12...HARMONY IS A DRUG

Horace was feeling sad, he had spoken with Waiehu by phone, and the Christmas catch up was not going to happen. She was snowed under with work. A cyclone was brewing in the Arafura Sea, which meant all hands on deck to lock down and secure specimens if required. Horace was now of two minds, hang around in Cairns or travel south to Brisbane then Sydney. The weather would determine outcomes.

Horace was on the flight to Cairns; the plane was being chased by storm clouds. He was sitting next to a Brisbane based psychiatrist, named Isiah Couche. Horace just offered his thought reinforcing smile:

"You're a psychiatrist, named Couche?"

Isiah was a short stocky man and was dressed in a tweed suit with a vest, bow tie and a Flat-Cap as a head warmer. To Horace he was definitely not a funeral director. Isiah had just attended a Darwin conference on gullibility. He told Horace that he spent his spare time studying cults. Isiah's ambition was to find the reason why cults have such a profound influence over normal people. A new interest arose when he heard about a secretive order called the *'Flautist Ladies.'* This was a small group of young northern New South Wales women musicians. They met twice yearly on a Nimbin Farm with their spiritual guide, a charismatic leader named Harmony. His real name was Simon Song, he was born in Hong Kong. His father was Chinese and his mother

English.

With Harmony's guidance, his ladies produced a combination of flute tones that they believe could expel evil parasites from their bodies. With medical terminology gleaned from Wikipedia on parasitic liver flukes, and his charismatic appeal, he had his followers convinced that parasites caused most if not all their maladies. As such, harmonic melodies, white wine and not eating raw or undercooked freshwater fish would bring balance back to their lives. That, and the fact he was a tall lean man and extremely good looking, with bright blue eyes and a soft hypnotising voice, led the easy manipulated ladies into servitude.

As a side benefit to Harmony, the combination of his followers flute tones blended into chords that pleased the soul. This soothing melody often led to sexual stimulation and group coitus whenever the opportunity arose. He also encouraged these flautist ladies to busk in malls and stations to raise money to help support his lifestyle. There was no coercion, they did it willingly. This cult became Isiah's focus group. The ladies had a common style, they dressed in long flowing coloured robes and they all wore their hair long and out.

Horace was astounded at the lives of some Australians.

"You're telling me that a fellow called Simon Song, whose flute playing nymphs call Harmony, is running a sex den in Nimbin off the budget of good-looking buskers."

"That's about it Horace."

"Now I have heard everything, I think I should have attended that gullibility conference as well Isiah."

"No, Horace these are facts."

Horace's notebook was filling fast. He liked Isiah and they exchanged contact details for a catch up in Brisbane. He was still thinking that Isiah's cult fantasies may be just a fabrication in the mind of a bored Psychiatrist, but he would keep an open mind about it. The plane landed in Cairns, it took a buffeting on the landing as the wind had picked up. He waved goodbye to his new Psychiatrist friend and made his way to the baggage pickup area. Adjacent to a car rental booth was a beautiful lady in a long dress playing a flute. That nailed it, Isiah wasn't kidding. Horace stood there listening to her haunting melodies, but didn't feel in the least bit sexually aroused, if anything he felt sorry for weak minds. He left *Penelope the weaver of charms'* a token dollar, but he knew Harmony would never thank him.

Later that day Penelope bought herself an ice-cream, using the special two-dollar coin that Waiehu had left, *(C... 'I'll miss that music.')*. The lady in Wendy's Creamery gave it in change to Seymore Black a coal miner from Peak Downs. Seymore bought a paper from Arnold Prescot the newsagent who gave it in change to Badri Patel, who bought a card for his mother. Badri was heading back to Woolgoolga to visit his family. He stopped at Townsville to buy some mangoes at a roadside stall and used his small change. Tom Howard, the Cairns *'Deals on Wheels'* franchise owner stopped at the same spot for the same reason and received the special coin in change. He put it in his fob pocket and drove on to Rockhampton for a pickup of O.P.J's, *'other people's junk'*, at a Council clean-up.

(C ... 'now I'm feeling used.')

* * *

Horace booked a night in a motel opposite the Cairns Esplanade Lagoon. After dropping off his bags he went out to buy a heavy-duty wind umbrella. A weather report said another cyclone was forming in the Coral Sea. The weather was definitely turning for the worse. He went for a walk and was astounded at the size of Cairns. The public swimming area set in parkland was one of the best layouts he had ever come across. People didn't swim in the bay for a few good reasons, they included the deadly box jellyfish called stingers, the tiny but deadly Irukandji jelly fish, sharks, and large saltwater crocodiles. The other reasons were; in World War two the Americans dredged the bay for war ships, and later on the Grafton shipping lane was created. The result was that the sandy beach was no more. It didn't bother Horace, there would be no swimming in this weather.

After the walk Horace retired to the hotel bar. He took the opportunity to write three post cards, this time he sent one to Waiehu as well. He detailed his Arnhem Land adventure and his thrilling flight. On Waiehu's he wrote a little extra about how much he was missing her. As he sat in the bar thinking about his next move, he saw some friendly faces that he recognised, it was Doug and Layla Pitt, and he caught their attention:

"There would be no fluttering on poker machines around here Digger"

"G'day Horace, no problem about pokies, there's a pub down the road and Layla has already wasted a quid. And how are you, seen many real estate agents?"

"No, I think they maybe escaping the cyclones. Except for the weather prediction, I'm well how about you?"

"We head out tomorrow, into the storm so to speak, a two-hour trip to Mount Carbine, population one hundred. My new job will be mining tungsten. The company provides a house, Layla comes from a small town, I think she will like it. The pub has two pokies and a pool table. Jokes aside the money is good. Where are you going next Horace?"

"The weather has changed my plans; I'm going to brave a rail trip to Kuranda tomorrow and hopefully come back on the sky rail. I've heard the bird sanctuary there is not to be missed. That will be about it, this incoming cyclone means I will be flying south very soon, I was hoping to visit Townsville and Fraser Island on my way to Brisbane, but I didn't factor in the Banshee cyclone."

There were two cyclones brewing, both possible category fives. They still had names not numbers. Cyclone Banshee was heading for Cairns, its name meant 'the screaming spirit'. The other one a bit further west, was now brooding off Cape York, and they called it Cyclone Dolores, 'the lady of sorrows'. After hearing the report; 'two days off Cairns,' on the radio, Horace walked out to a sunny day and the wind had dropped. He caught a cab to the Scenic Railway; it ran from Cairns over the Great Dividing Range to the town of Kuranda on the Atherton Tableland. This was all part of the World Heritage Barron Gorge National Park in Queensland's wet tropics.

On arrival he was amazed, there was so much to do, a Butterfly Sanctuary, a Koala Garden, the Bird World, and a pub for lunch. Horace was in a great mood and hopefully the rain would hold off. He wouldn't have time for white water rafting and waterfalls. The Bird World was a treat, there were over 350 birds roaming freely in their beautiful rainforest habitat. Horace found himself having a conversation with Henry, a yellow crested cockatoo and his girlfriend Nancy. They were a couple of cheeky in-house residents. After chasing butterflies, getting peed on by a Koala and then devouring a burger and beer at the pub, Horace was ready to head back to Cairns. The Sky Rail Rainforest Cableway was over seven kilometres of pure joy. He got back to the motel just as the rain started to fall. It would be on and off like this for the next six months.

'*Noah would be building his ark about now,*' thought Horace.

He decided to give Townsville a miss and the next day he was off to Hervey Bay.

* * *

There would be no Christmas on Lizard Island this year, Cyclone Banshee,' *the screaming spirit,*' lived up to its name. Waiehu was reading the postcard from Horace, trying to take her mind off the howling destruction taking place outside her unit in the shelter. She recalled the message on that coin, '*love is a currency, spend it wisely.*' She was wise beyond her years and wanted her career more than love at that stage. This didn't mean she couldn't spend a little on the way and Horace was worth it.

The island structures were built to withstand a category five, but everything, including Waiehu were shaking by the storm force. She could hear the crashing sounds of uprooted palms and torn off sheets of roofing outside. The site manager Justin Casey had been through this before, last time the repair bill was fifty million dollars, this one would cost more. The structures might survive but everything else would be stripped to oblivion. Justin had already arranged transfers for staff. It would be six months before they could return. Waiehu was organised for a short-term transfer to the marine biology department at Brisbane University to study coral reef ecology. She was of two minds, she would miss the close-up study on this beautiful isle, but six months in Brisbane meant she could now spend Christmas with Horace, who she also missed.

CHAPTER 13...A DINGO HAS MY AKUBRA

Horace needed his umbrella to get to his four-wheel drive hire car at Hervey Bay airport. He had booked a ferry trip and two nights at Kingfisher Bay Resort on Fraser Island. He had read about the Aboriginal and naming history of Fraser Island on the flight from Cairns. Its real name is K'gari, it had been called that for five thousand years by the Butchulla people. They were the people of the sea, and their totem was that of a dolphin. The English Island name came from an Eliza Fraser, who was shipwrecked there in 1836.

Fraser Island has a World Heritage status, and its wildest inhabitants are the dingoes. They have called this sandy island home for thousands of years, as such they are protected. Adult dingoes are about the size of a medium dog but unlike dogs, dingoes don't bark they howl like wolves. They love to swim, spend a lot of time on the beach walking and chasing English tourists for food.

Horace wanted to make the best of his brief time on Fraser Island. He had an early night at the resort and after breakfast headed straight for the centre of the island. There were heavy clouds overhead and occasional showers, but in his four-wheel drive he managed to get to the various places on the tourist map. The freshwater lake in the centre of the island was a wonder of nature. He finally made his way to a secluded area of beach. The sun peaked through a break in the clouds and the white sand glistened, all was still and inviting. The sand was soft under foot, so he grabbed his thermos of tea and a cut sandwich lunch and went for a walk to sit at the water's edge.

There wasn't another soul about as he sat there looking at that pristine island wilderness. The only indication of humans were the tyre tracks in the sand. He heard a howl, it sounded like a wolf, but he knew better. Dingoes were pack animals and took advantage of situations when there was an opportunity to have a free meal. Horace heard a soft growl and turned to look behind him, he was now staring into the eyes of a full-size adult male dingo. He wasn't sure what to do, so, he grabbed his thermos and thought that might make a good weapon. He threw the remainder of his sandwich at the dog, and it scoffed it down so quick that Horace was thinking he may be the next nibble.

He decided to follow the park warning sign advice to walk quickly away from the situation. As he did, the sun disappeared, and the wind picked up. His Akubra flew off back towards what was now a pack of dingoes. One of the younger ones grabbed it and took off into the scrub, it wasn't playing fetch. Horace didn't know what to do, if he chased it, he might end up like the sandwich. He took the safe option and went back to the car. His mood darkened a bit, like the overhead storm clouds, so he decided to go back to the resort and spend his last night by the bar.

He was back in his funeral outfit and wearing the Derby Bowler again, it was his 'Linus Blanket' outfit when feeling lonely. While polishing off his second schooner, his phone rang, it was Waiehu. She was in tears over the call for evacuation of the island. Horace was empathetic, but when she spoke of the temporary transfer to the

University of Queensland in Brisbane for six months, and a possible catch up for Christmas, his mood suddenly improved. He suggested that they could meet up in a South Bank motel, and perhaps have a few days together, she agreed. Horace went to bed that night feeling a little bit guilty over his happiness, while Waiehu was going through that distress.

The next day he travelled back to the airport at Hervey Bay, he was feeling elated. He wasn't thinking about cyclones, dingoes and Akubra hats anymore, he was thinking of Waiehu and the future. While at the airport he bought her a Christmas present, it was an artistic depiction of Yul'lu the Butchulla dolphin totem, and he knew she would love it.

CHAPTER 14...A BRISBANE AFFAIR

I siah Couche was adjacent to the taxi terminal in Brisbane Airport listening to another pretty flautist whose name tag said 'Cassandra who shines.' Horace came up behind him:

"They're like mushrooms Isiah, they pop up everywhere."

"G'day Horace! How was Cairns?"

"Loved the visit to Karanda, but the pending cyclones have sent me south earlier than I had expected. I stopped off at Fraser Island, fed the dingoes my new Akubra, and escaped without making the news story of the day, what about you?"

"You must watch those precious K9's, they are partial to tourists and at least they didn't get your Derby Bowler. As for me I'm heading home, my wife has been hounding me to return. We just built a granny flat extension to earn some extra cash, and she has done most of the fit out. I'm not in her good books. Where are you going next?"

"That's a hard one, for the time being it's a motel on the South Bank. A friend of mine is coming to Brisbane because of the cyclone damage up north. She has a temporary deployment to the University of Queensland for six months. I hope to get to know her a bit better, and you can take my meaning literally."

"Ah! young love is a wonderful thing." He laughed.

"Horace, you must watch out in that South Brisbane area, with these rain depressions coming we could be in for more Brisbane River flooding. The views of the flooding from the motel may be good, but you may get stuck there. Tell your lady friend that I will give her a fair price to rent our new granny flat, if she wishes. We live in Barton up near the Botanical Gardens, it's only a ten-minute drive to the University, and way above the flood waters. You have my number."

"Thank you Isiah, I will let her know. If she takes up the offer it means I might be seeing more of you, and I can learn some more about your cult investigations."

Horace headed off to the motel thinking he might just stay in Brisbane a bit longer than he intended.

Heavy rain clouds followed Waiehu all the way to Brisbane airport. She had arranged to meet Horace at the Mantra on the South Bank around four. The conversation with the taxi driver was all about the rising river:

"If Brisbane goes under again, it will be the third time in as many years, I'm over this rain. My ground floor has been flooded out twice now and we thought we were safe. My wife will be crying again tonight."

"I'm sorry, you never know maybe this time it will not be as bad."

Waiehu's empathy was all she could offer, but she did give him a good tip. People were still doing it tough. When she arrived, she thanked the driver and wished him well. Standing at the door of the Mantra was Horace with a smile as wide as the gateway to Luna Park. Waiehu hugged him and gave him a welcoming kiss on the cheek. They exchanged some small talk of her escape from cyclone carnage and the approaching harsh weather. He then helped her check into a room near his:

"I have booked dinner at the Japanese restaurant just two blocks away, an under awning walk, if that's ok. I will let you settle in and see you in two hours."

"Thanks Horace, that is appreciated," she smiled.

Horace, ever the gentleman had a lot to say, but for now he thought it wise to let her rest before dinner. He was a little nervous, so he went to the motel bar for a drink and a think.

When Horace knocked on her door at six, Waiehu looked stunning. She was dressed in tightly fitting jeans and a soft pink blouse. Horace wore his suit pants, with an open neck striped shirt. He left his coat and bowler hat in the bag this time. Waiehu seemed impressed with his appearance, she thought he was a handsome and refined man. Although it was still raining, it wasn't cold, they both felt comfortable. She held his hand as they walked to the restaurant, Horace had one of those infatuated schoolboy tremors. The last time this happened, he was having a dance at the Cotswold Grammar School formal with Mabel Fobsworth. She was Beryl's sister, the better looking of the pair and branded as the school stunner. She told him he was clumsy for stepping on her toes. Horace was not experienced at dating and thankfully neither was Waiehu.

The Japanese food was delicious. Horace had never had Japanese food before, and Waiehu told him what dishes she thought he would enjoy the most. Waiehu then went on to tell him all about the island experience and cyclone damage. She had just been through her introductory course and was told her research portfolio was to be associated with the extent of coral bleaching, and the 'Crown of Thorns' star fish problems, when the evacuation was made mandatory. Horace felt for her, she was a dedicated professional. He told her of his adventures in Arnhem land and the thrilling flight with Plane Bob. He had her crying with laughter and wonder, all the while soaking up the loveliness of her being. After dinner they found their way back to the motel bar for coffees. Horace told her about the furnished granny flat offer from Isiah and she was keen:

"That's ideal Horace, I have been a little worried about my next move. I can stay here for a few days, but I must buy a get-around secondhand car and organise my courses."

"Well, I'm stuck here with the inclement weather, and a beautiful friend for a while, so why don't I help you find a car tomorrow and we can share the fuel cost to visit some of the local sites? I will also call Isaiah tomorrow and tell him we can drive out and have a look at the flat. What's your thoughts?"

"That's great Horace, you are such a gentleman. I also know some great spots around here to show you, have you ever seen Gondwanaland Antarctic beech trees?"

"No, I can't say I have, but knowing you, I'm in for another surprise."

"The Springbrook National Park is recognised as part of one of the world's most outstanding and valuable places. The vegetation found there is the most ancient in Australia. It's beautiful in the rain and it's only a two-hour drive from here."

"You are amazing!"

She kissed him on the cheek, said good night, and

went to her room. Horace was still uncertain where this relationship was heading, but for now he was still on a high.

They spent half of the next day searching for a car. Waiehu finally got a good deal on a late model Hyundai, and they drove out to Isaiah's house to look at the flat. Esmeralda Couche answered the door, Waiehu and Horace introduced themselves. First meetings are often shy, but Esmeralda was a whirl wind of happiness. Horace thought her appearance synchronised with her name. She was originally from the Ukraine, but had the looks of a Romani palm reader, with long flowing red hair, earrings the size of hubcaps and eye lashes that you could sweep the floor with. She was a foot taller than her husband Isiah who stood behind her, and she spoke with a Ukrainian accent, but she was as sweet as honey and welcomed them in. They lived alone; their children all lived interstate. It was written on their faces that they loved to have company.

The flat was just what Waiehu wanted. She told Isiah that she would love to move in that week. It was only three days before Christmas, but Isiah and Esmeralda were not concerned.

"What's your plans for Christmas?" Esmeralda asked.

"As yet we have no plans." Responded Horace.

"Well in that case, please be our guests, I will prepare a Christmas feast of welcome. Do you have any cuisine issues and specific requirements?"

Waiehu clapped with excitement and Horace nodded with agreement. They both felt comfortable with this couple.

"In Bourton-on-the-Water Christmas was a village affair," laughed Horace. "If it snowed, we would get the sleds out, put the mittens and scarves on and have fun."

"Well, I can assure you there will be no snow, just rain, but we will have lots of fun."

Cyclone Banshee *'the screaming spirit'* and Cyclone Dolores, *'the lady of sorrows,'* joined forces in Cairns and the wall of water was heading south, with major flooding events. The rain would not give up, there were minor flooding reports for the Brisbane River and further south, Northern New South Wales was in for another soaking. The Richmond and Clarence rivers were on full flood alert and Lismore for the third time in recent years, was facing disaster.

Waiehu and Horace spent one more night in the motel. She asked Horace if he could stay with her for a while after Christmas, until she settled in at the flat. He agreed that it would be good to get to know the Couches a little better before he continued his journey. That last night was a watershed in their budding relationship. Horace took the opportunity and gave Waiehu an early Christmas present, the artistic depiction of Yul'lu the Butchulla dolphin totem. This brought tears to her eyes, they glistened with happiness as she remembered their dolphin encounter at Monkey Mia. After a lovely meal and a few drinks at a Steak House, they retired to the door of Waiehu's room, where for the first time they kissed. From that point they created their own cyclone. Both were novices in the art of intimacy but managed to fulfill their inner needs. They slept the night together and woke to a new world and many decisions to make. After breakfast, they packed their gear into the Hyundai and dropped it off at Couche's granny flat and then headed to Springbrook National Park. The river near the motel was just reaching the tops of the levee banks, it was a suitable time to head for higher ground.

Springbrook's top attractions were the ancient Beech Trees in the Gondwana rainforest, the Purling Brook Falls, and the Natural Arch rock formation which was a cascading waterfall over a basalt cave. All involved short walks, and the best time to see them was right after rainfall, and they had plenty of that. Horace once again was in awe of this country's natural wonders and the knowledge of his special new friend and lover.

CHAPTER 15...SHE'LL BE RIGHT MATE

J ack Wright and his family had lived in the suburb of Redcliffe near Brisbane for the last 40 years. Jack a mechanic by trade, was locally known as a motorhead, he loved his cars, especially Fords. When he wasn't tinkering under the bonnet of his Mustang GT, you would find him watching the car racing on TV or taking his son to a local meet. His favourite car was the Ford Shelby, a high-performance Mustang, named after a Texas chicken farmer, turned race car driver Carroll Shelby.

Jack and his wife Cheryl had only one son and in keeping with Jack's love of cars he named his son Shelby. It was a unisex name, but rare in Australia. Shelby was a bright boy but had a touch of learning difficulty. When he reached high school, his name earnt him many tags. *'She'll-be-right'* received the biggest laughs. He left school in year nine after struggling with attention issues and worked with his father for a while. Shelby had his own life plans; he made a bit of money selling what he called O.P.Js, *'other people's junk'*. He had found a skill at which he was quite adept. His father set him up in a Pawnshop business that he worked for ten years. The shop bought goods from the disposable income economy of the local struggler for next to nothing and resold them at higher prices.

Shelby had an entrepreneur's business brain and expanded his purchases. The company Pantech's were bright green and painted on the side with the words:

'Shelby Wright- Deals on Wheels- She'll be Right Mate.'

Eventually the tagline *'Deals on Wheels'* became a business franchise. There was good money to be made visiting markets, deceased estates and even off-the-street council pick-ups. Shelby was never without a quid. Occasionally on the runs to deceased estates, they picked up real bargains and the profits were staggering. Although he had a poor education Shelby was a street wise businessman and he knew the expression, *'she'll be right mate,'* would always help a sale.

He had grown into a tall, well-built street wise man, who could manage anything life threw at him, including punches. With his hard-earned wealth, Shelby invested wisely. He purchased a two-hundred-acre property at Nimbin in northern New South Wales and built a large retreat and storage centre. He loved the laid-back hippy atmosphere of the town and its access north and south of the border. What he didn't know at the time, was that a kilometre away, nestled well off the road was Simon Songs flautist cult farm.

* * *

The few days of intimacy at the Couche's granny flat, blew out to two weeks. Waiehu and Horace were making the best of their time together. They both knew that the relationship could only be sporadic over the next few years. They had commitments and career choices to deal with. That night the Couches invited them to dinner again. They walked over to the main house holding hands. Esmeralda Couche answered the door in her usual

Romani attire. Horace could smell a stew cooking, but when he looked in the kitchen there was no cauldron and Hansel and Gretel didn't come running out. Horace was in a jolly mood. Isiah was sitting in the lounge room smoking a pipe and reading a book about Charles Manson. Esmeralda gave Waiehu a kiss on the cheek and started talking about her herb garden, which now was her main hobby following her former career in botany at the adjacent Botanical Gardens.

Over a delicious dinner and two bottles of shiraz they exchange some discussions on climate change, the present La Nina event, and the devastating floods in Lismore. After dinner the ladies retired to the kitchen and the men to the lounge room, as is the custom in a Romani coven. Although the men did offer to clear the table and wipe up.

"I would love to learn some more about your flautist cult investigations Isiah?"

"Well, I have an offer for you. There is a music festival being planned next week at Nimbin, to raise funds for the Lismore flood victims. A local businessman named Shelby Wright, is sponsoring the event, he runs a company called 'Deals on Wheels.' Shelby has a large property on which the event will be held and it is not far from Simon Songs cult headquarters. Why don't you join me? We could get some good intel and listen to some music at the same time."

"That sounds great Isiah, Waiehu starts at the University next week and its time I continued my journey south. 'Finding Earth Magazine' editor has been on my back about progress of late."

"Then its settled, I will book us into a short stay

cabin near there and get tickets to the festival. I would bet money on it, that the flute ladies make an appearance."

The night ended on a high note, with shots of vodka, and Esmeralda singing Ukrainian love songs.

Waiehu was not bothered by the news that Horace would be leaving soon. Their relationship was one of love and respect for each other and their careers. They talked it out and decided that they would rekindle their desires whenever possible. They spoke of visits to England and Japan, and even Barrier Reef Island escapes from time to time. They knew each other's needs in a sexual way were not the big issues present in the lives of many. They also knew that one day in the future, they would be together on a more permanent basis. The question would be location.

They had two more nights of the big intimacy issues present in the lives of many, then parted ways with hugs and kisses. Esmeralda and Waiehu waved goodbye as their men drove off in Isiah's Volkswagen. It was still raining. Isiah saw that Horace had a sad look on his face about leaving his one true love. The psychiatrist's analysis came to the fore, with the words:

"She will be alright mate; life is all about direction and choices."

CHAPTER 16...DIAMONDS IN THE SKY

Shane and Clarissa Huckster, the rich American jewellery merchants that Horace had met in Walpole, had continued their journey from Ballarat. They took in all the best country hospitality on offer. They went for a Murray River cruise at Echuca, then stopped at Parkes to see the famous Telescope, used when Armstrong walked on the moon. They hiked the Breadknife at the Warrumbungle National Park and sang with country music stars in Tamworth. They drove on through the high country to Armidale and then onto Tenterfield and the Gwydir Highway back to the coast via Casino.

They left Tenterfield in the late morning, hoping to reach Byron Bay before dark. This day of their Australian adventure kicked off listening to a Peter Allan song, 'I still call Australia home.' They couldn't agree more, they both loved the place and were considering moving here permanently after this latest delivery. Again, they took their time and underestimated the distance to travel. They were on the Bruxner Highway approaching Lismore, it was getting dark, and pouring with rain. It had been a long drive on the winding two lane highway. They had stopped at Casino for lunch and afternoon drinks at a pub, and both were getting tired, and Clarissa forgot to put her seatbelt on.

With heavy rains the Wilson River is a mighty force of water. From the higher country south of the

Queensland border with New South Wales, this river flows to Coraki where it meets up with the Richmond River. It then travels on a long meander to the Pacific Ocean at Ballina. In times of flood, land around Coraki looks like an inland sea. At Gundurimba the Wilson River was only metres from the road and the river height was peaking. Clarissa was sound asleep and Shane could not have picked a worse place to doze off. A Beatles track, *'Lucy in the sky with diamonds'*, was softly playing on the car stereo system and Shane was mind driving through the autumn-coloured forest in New York State. The trouble was he was on an Australian road and in the wrong lane when the semi-trailer came around the bend. To the sound of emergency breaking and the words:

'Picture yourself in a boat on a river with tangerine trees and marmalade skies,'

The semi jack-knifed, clipped the Huckster's car and like a bat on ball, helped the car on its journey into the river. Clarissa, it turned out was the lucky one, her door flew open and she was launched into a tree. Shane was now wide awake upside down in the car floating down the flooding Wilson River, and water was pouring in. Shane was struggling to get his seatbelt off, but sadly drowned. His life washed out of him as the car sank and the luggage departed downstream. The driver of the semi was trapped but uninjured, he managed the triple zero call, and within minutes he could hear the Ambulance and Police rescue squad coming.

When they arrived the Paramedics found Clarissa and helped free the semi driver who pointed to the scrub and direction that the car had travelled. The Police found no sign of the car at the river's edge and called in the S.E.S back up crews to help locate it. Clarissa was unconscious, had suffered a broken arm and a serious cracked skull. She was taken to Lismore Base Hospital. The highway was blocked for three hours while the road carnage was cleared and the police forensic staff assessed the accident for the coroner. It took two days to locate the car, Shane was still in the front seat.

Clarissa was later transferred to Brisbane Hospital and laid there in a coma for a month. Her brother came out from Boston and had her transferred back to the States. It would be three more months before she became aware of Shanes fate. She missed the funeral and memorial for Shane, and was devastated for another reason as well, the special water bottles were now lost in an Australian flood.

* * *

The fund-raising music festival was being organised to help the residents of Coraki as much as Lismore and Shelby Wright had organised the local Councils and the Byron Bay community to help. These were the fourth major flood in as many years and the remaining residence in Lismore and Coraki were in dire straits. Shelby's company had become wealthy from the franchises over the past few years, and now was the time to give some back to the strugglers and those in the low-income society. His warehouses were full of the things people needed to rebuild their lives, and his Nimbin property storage facility was the main hub of the business. He called the charity:

'She'll be right mate; we are here to help.'

It was a philanthropic venture that blended well

with the Australian ethos of helping out in troubled times.

Shelby was organising for two more of the companies 'Deals on Meals' trucks to be there on the day. They would be stationed around the festival site to sell specific items for the charity. Free household essential items from the farm storage facility would be handed out with proof of need. All the money from all sales and festival tickets was to be donated to the fund raiser. Cairns franchise owner Tom Howard had just picked up a load of household goods in Rockhampton and was on his way south. Kyle Driver the franchise owner from Coffs Harbour was heading north. Shelby was covering all their expenses for the effort. Kyle's truck was full of basic household items as well.

Shelby didn't have any contacts in Coraki, but he had asked Kyle to check out the situation there on the way through. Kyle was driving east of Coraki following the high ground along Wyrallah Road towards Tuki Tuki Nature reserve. The rain was constant as he stopped at a high ridge at the end of Wyrallah Road. Looking west, all he could see was flooded land. He was seeing the devastation through binoculars and noticed some objects washed up on the riverbank, just below the ridge adjacent to Ramsay's Canal. He managed to drop down the embankment to the water's edge and fish out assorted items of luggage which included two muddied up day packs with wet weather gear, and two water bottles.

Kyle had heard about the Huckster's accident on the radio. He thought about letting the police know about the gear but changed his mind. One drowned American and one in a coma, wouldn't care too much about some muddied up and water-soaked backpack gear. Besides that, there was no wallets, money or anything of real value in the packs. They would probably fetch a few dollars for charity at the festival.

CHAPTER 17...COIN KARMA

Scott Bannister lived for most of his miserable life in Ettalong on the Central Coast. At school he achieved the barest of education in a learning difficulty class, in which he was branded as a bully. On the rugby league paddock, he was a thug and sent off constantly. After a teenage life of picking fights, sometimes with tougher men, he carried some scars. They were not all external, the internal ones had made him nasty. In later life he was no oil painting to look at. He only once managed to attract a girlfriend, but he was so possessive and controlling, she left him after a brief time. Finally, he grew up a bit and found a job after being essentially a Centre Link recipient for ten years. The only work that suited him was as a standover man for a Debt Collector agency. In short, Scrags, as he was known by the boys at the Woy Woy pub, was a real lowlife who swam in the shallow end of the gene pool, as did his only friend, and room-mate Pimple, real name Peter Simple. They shared a two-bedroom shack in Blackwall, about two klicks from their Woy Woy pub.

Pimple was a better looking bloke, who had no problems smooth talking certain women. The trouble was, it was always about lust, not love. His biggest life issue was lack of education. He left school at fourteen and lived at home with his separated alcoholic mum. They had a huge fight on his eighteenth birthday, so he moved in with Scrags. He still visited his mum occasionally, mainly to collect his pot crop. Unknown to her, he made some spending money by growing marijuana in the middle of his mum's would-be-if-it-could-be vegetable garden. She thought they were just weeds. Having a mate like Scrags meant Pimple's destiny looked like it was set in concrete. Then one day in the bar he met a Greek girl named Reeya Lambros, she was attractive and her smile would melt butter. Something about the way Peter admired her sparked her ego. For Peter Simple, it was one of the few times in his life that a pretty girl smiled at him, he was smitten.

Reeya lived and worked in North Sydney. They had a short chat and exchanged addresses and social media info. Reeya was going to Greece for six months, to settle some family estate issues. She would send an occasional picture, which was the extent of her involvement. Pimple bragged about her when talking to his mate Scrags. This didn't stop his eyes from wandering, he was not one for love at a distance, even if the love was all in his mind.

Scott was a contract worker for a company called Cash-Hope. They had links to the shady side of the lending market. The after payments for extended default could lead to hospitalisation and sometimes even worse. One defaulter was currently under scrutiny and in six months of arrears. Several letters and emails had been sent to Mr Song of Harmony Inc., but no response had been received. Scrags was sent north to Nimbin to encourage repayment and if possible, recoup the debt. He offered his mate Pimple an unpaid holiday to Nimbin, in part to share the driving. Pimple jumped at the opportunity:

"Hippy chicks and drugs Scrags, my kind of vacation."

"Not only that Pimps, there's a music festival on up there, and all those Byron Bay babes will be there as well."

* * *

Horace and Isiah had a couple of days before the festival, so they decided to travel the back road through Mount Warning and then down the Blue Knob Road to Nimbin. There were still the occasional showers and road repair stoppages, but Horace loved the drive. The idyllic green hills and granite rock vistas were a delight. As per usual he was bemused by Australia's place naming. He looked at Isiah:

"Why on Earth would they call an extinct volcanic caldera, Mount Warning, it's already blown to smithereens," he laughed, "and, what's a Blue Knob?"

"Well, my learned Cotswoldian friend, Mount Warning's name had nothing to do with warning of a pending volcanic eruption, it was named by James Cook in 1770, as a maritime hazard indicator for dangerous offshore reefs. As for the Blue Knob, it's a type of granite. When Mount Warning erupted some twenty odd million years back, it left a series of jagged outcrops and solidified plugs. When these volcanic dykes and vents, on the flanks of the volcano eroded, we were left with a marketable building product."

"Wow! Isiah, how is it a cult researching psychiatrist knows so much geology?"

"Simple, Wikipedia and Google."

As they drove along, they were listening to some soft classical music on Radio National. A special news bulletin came on and mentioned that two American tourists were in a tragic car accident with a semi-trailer just outside Lismore. One drowned in the flooded Wilson River and the other was taken to Lismore Base Hospital in a coma. Relatives in Boston were being notified.

"What a terrible thing to happen on a holiday." Said Isiah.

"Yes it's horrific," replied Horace, "I met a nice couple in Walpole, they were from Boston also, I truly hope it wasn't them. No, it couldn't be, they told me they were heading to Sydney.'

The concerts wouldn't get under way until Saturday, so our music loving cult investigators had two days to kill. They settled into their cabin on the outskirts of Nimbin, they would not be camping on site with hippies and mud. The next day after a quiet night and a local pizza, they headed to the village. It was very humid and overcast so Horace dressed in his khaki safari outfit. Even Isiah got out of the tweeds. He looked more like a golfer on a muck up day, a Hawaiian shirt, bright green shorts, long socks, and sandals.

Nimbin is a tourist hotspot; they get around 160,000 visitors each year. It is a type of commune town, where the locals have ownership of many of the important community buildings, sporting grounds and halls. The spirit and energy of the community is always visible in the artworks which can be found in almost every nook and cranny of the village. They have been embracing alternative lifestyles and sustainable living for over fourty years. Today many are what you could call Hippy land barons, some are quite wealthy. The village is very open with eco-tourism, colourful shops, and cafes that play off the alternative hippie image. Isiah gave

Horace the run down and history for his notes:

"Back in the 1840's they cleared all the wonderful cedar forests for homes in England and probably the Cotswolds. Today it is well known for its alternative culture. In the seventies it attracted a community of alternate life-stylers. Cannabis is openly sold and somewhat tolerated in Nimbin, although it's still illegal. You may think that the village is more about selling marijuana, than exploring alternative lifestyles, but you are unlikely to get hassled. If you look like you might be in the pot market, you may get an offer but if you refuse, you will politely be left alone. The nature of the town can mean that it isn't as innocent as many other New South Wales country towns of he same size. Tourists have been the victims of assaults in Nimbin. Take care if you decide to have a joint," Chuckled Isiah, "I'll be in the Café across the road."

"And I will be there with you Doc, tea and beer are my pleasures."

Both men ordered, Isiah had a flat white and Horace a pot of tea. They noticed a parked Volkswagen Combi van painted in peace symbols and psychedelic colours. A group of people were heading from the van to a shelter in the War Memorial Park adjacent to the Museum. There were four ladies dressed in flowing-coloured robes sitting in a circle around a tall man dressed in what looked like cricket whites. He had long hair and a beard to match.

"Jesus, Isiah, I think our flautist cult ladies and their leader are in town."

"Yes, but it's not Jesus, just a look-alike messiah they call Harmony, aka Simon Song."

With those words, a beautiful harmony of flute

music began. They both sat there, sipping their beverages mesmerized by the sound.

"I recognise two of those women Isiah."

"Yes, both were wearing name tags, they are *'Penelope the weaver'* from Cairns, and *'Cassandra who shines'* from Brisbane, and that's probably Simon Song. The other two ladies I don't know."

Isiah finished his coffee, left Horace with his second cup of tea. It was time for some in-depth research questions. He started to head across the road, and then suddenly stopped and returned to his seat. Two men had pulled up at the park and started to confront Mr Song.

✳ ✳ ✳

Scott Bannister and Peter Simple had arrived in Nimbin in an old Ute the Cash-Hope debt agency had leant them for the journey. Pimple was first to spot the women:

"Check out the chicks over there Scrags, they're playing flutes."

"We're in luck Pimps, that's the bloke we are here to see, he runs some sort of cult. Let's go over and give him the message, you keep your mouth shut and let me do the talking."

There wasn't much talking, it was a straight to the point encounter. The girls stopped playing and sat motionless. Simon was flustered by the onslaught and just stood there while Scrags tapped him on the chest with his finger:

"You   owe   Cash-Hope   twenty-thousand-two-hundred- and-sixty-two-dollars mate, and they want it now! They have been trying to contact you for six months, and they reckon you're ignoring them. How about we march over to the bank now and get it."

Simon was nervous with the threats but tried to reason with the thugs:

"I can get you ten thousand tomorrow and give you a guarantee that I will get back on track with the payments from now on. I have had some cash flow problems with the business. I recently got scammed and had to change phone numbers and email addresses, I'm sorry I forgot to tell your company."

"No point sucking up to me with paltry excuses, I'll check with the company to see if they're ok with your offer. Stay here don't move, Pimple will be here while I go and make the call, don't make me come chasing you."

The ladies were starting to cry, Simon although in shock, comforted them:

"It's all fine girls, just a misunderstanding."

Scrags came back, still in a threatening mood, Pimple had sat the whole time just leering at the ladies:

"You're in luck sport, just give me your new contact email and phone number and have that ten grand ready for pick up tomorrow. And don't get into arrears again, next time I won't be so pleasant."

Simon didn't want these two creeps coming out to his farm for the money. He had enough cash in his safe to pay the debt twenty times over, but he wasn't about to tell these two clowns that:

"The girls are playing at the festival tomorrow, can we meet you there, near the Blues stage at say 11am? I have a friend who will help with the cash."

The Woy Woy terrors were happy with that; it was just the excuse they needed to get Cash-Hope to pay for their entry.

"That was an easy extraction Pimps, lets head across to Byron for lunch and a look see."

Horace and Isiah saw the thugs leave and went over to talk to the group. They were all still shaking and appreciated a bit of empathy. Simon didn't elaborate on the encounter; he just said it was a business discussion. Isiah, smiled at the girls, Penelope and Cassandra recognised him, so he took the opportunity to talk about Harmony Inc. After chatting with Simon, Isiah started to get the impression that this wasn't a cult at all. He had been studying cult behavioural patterns for years. It seemed that urban myth and parasite removal techniques may all have had a roll in this companies image, for deflection purposes. Simon and his girls just played along with the scam. It turned out that there were only four girls in the group. They were all infatuated with Simon and the sexual activity was probably mutually agreeable, but there was something more in the way they bought the income in. Isaiah now had his suspicions, but it was obvious four flautist busking ladies were not wealth creators. Isiah and Horace discussed it and both came to the same conclusion.

"Drug distribution, from the Harmony Inc farm, probably weed or ice." Isiah told Horace.

"I will call the police when I get home, no sense wrecking their business until after the festival. We get to hear their beautiful music just one more time. The bad news is, I will have to find another cult now, hopefully one with more hypnotical ritualistic sacrifices."

Horace just smiled, "I will bet the women aren't as pretty, and make sure they don't have fangs after midnight."

* * *

Tom Howard arrived in Nimbin in the afternoon. The plan was for a massage, a drive to the warehouse to pack the gear for tomorrow's festival, then back to Nimbin pub for dinner and a beer. He parked his *'Deals on Wheels'* truck behind the town massage parlour owned and operated by Sky Lovejoy and called, *'Lovejoy's Massage'*. A one-hour remedial massage was just what he needed after the long drive. He was her first customer of the day. He stripped off, threw his clothes over a chair and laid on the massage bed. The two-dollar coin dropped out of is fob pocket onto the floor.

(C... thank heaven, I was getting claustrophobic in there)

Tom always stopped off for a massage when he came to Shelby's Nimbin Warehouse. He was quite friendly with Sky, and she was a good therapist. She had her work cut out with him, he was a huge man, all sinew and muscle, with a few scars from past fights. In his younger days he was a heavyweight amateur boxer. Sky had a lot of personal problems, mostly man trouble. She liked Tom, he was a gentle giant, and he always gave her a good tip. Sky's next appointment after Tom was due around four. He was someone she didn't know, an out of towner named Peter Simple. She thought he was a bit weird, he said she could call him Pimple. She needed the income, so despite reservation she booked him in.

After Tom left, Sky sat on the bed and thought about her last boyfriend Midge. He lived in Byron Bay on the dole and spent his life surfing. He was low on life prospects, but she loved him. She noticed the coin on the carpet, picked it up and saw the inscription. *'Love is a currency, spend it wisely.'* That brought tears to her eyes, one thing she had never done was to spend love wisely.

(C...*I hate these sad encounters*)

Sky placed the coin on the sideboard and left the room, she had a Yoga class before the afternoon appointment.

After a day of sniffing around Byron Bay perving on the lady talent, Scrags and Pimple headed back to Nimbin. Pimple got dropped off for his massage and Scrags headed for the pub. Sky was a bit reluctant at first, when she saw how dishevelled this Pimple person appeared. She told him about the cost for a torso remedial massage, and he elected a half hour. She told him to remove his upper clothing and she left the room. When she returned, he was lying face down fully naked. From the very start it was obvious Pimple had expected more:

"I'm not sure if you are aware but this is a therapeutic remedial massage establishment Mr Simple. If you require something more, you will have to go elsewhere."

He was charged up now and not willing to give up so easily. He then touched and groped her. Sky had had enough, she gave him a bloody nose with a quick right hook and showed him the door:

"Get dressed Mr Simple, this is not a brothel."

"I'll go when I get my money's worth bitch!"

"No! you will go now or the next blow will be your crutch."

Pimple was stunned by the blow and the threat; he got off the bed and shoved Sky backwards to the floor and started to put his clothes back on. She left him there to change. He looked around the room thinking to cause some damage and saw some coins on the side table.

'At least the bitch can do is buy me a beer,' he thought, as he shoved the coins into his pocket. He barged out the door back onto the street. Sky was shaken by the encounter, but she had experienced worse yobbo's in her life.

* * *

Horace and Isaiah went back to the cabin to change for dinner. Later in the afternoon they headed back to the Nimbin hotel for a meal. They dressed back into their Sunday best. No ties, just open neck shirts, good trousers, and the Derby Bowler and Flat cap. Management had a bouncer on the front door, who looked them up and down. He had a tag on that said:

'Jake Carter, my trouble is your trouble.'

They were being cautious with an out-of-town crowd coming in for the festival. As they walked into the hotel the mostly hippy crowd looked on in wonder. The sun was still trying to escape the clouds, and they sat on the back veranda. It was a beautiful treescape garden and very tropical. In a typical Nimbin fashion, there was a humpy shed on the back lawn, called the *'Cannabis Jungle'*. It looked like it was built in ten minutes by students floating in an LSD dream. It was obvious that it was specially designed for smoking marijuana and the décor didn't matter.

The pub was packed but the *'Cannabis Jungle'* was empty, it had the look of a post-midnight hangout. It seemed that quite a few people came up early for the weekend festival and decided to have dinner at the hotel as well. Horace and Isaiah sat there chatting about Horace's next place to visit:

"I've decided to check out Byron Bay, then move on to Sydney via Nambucca Heads and Nelson Bay. They're the three coastal spots that seem to get talked about by my English friends. When I get back to Sydney, I booked into a B&B in Milsons Point. I have tickets for a show there, the *'Complete works of Shakespeare in a hundred minutes'*, it's a comedy of errors so to speak. Really looking forward to it, it's at the Kirribilli Theatre. I might even pop in for a beer with the Prime Minister while I'm there."

Isiah was now starting to get use to Horace's occasional absurdities and banter.

When he went to get a shout, Horace heard a ruckus coming from the pool table area. He noticed the two fellows in the pool room were the same two thugs who accosted Simon Song that afternoon. They both seemed well on their way to being quite inebriated. Horace avoided them; he wasn't prepared to give his judo green belt a workout. Tom Howard and his boss Shelby Wright then walked out onto the pub veranda. They looked at the two strange guys with the funny hats and sat down on the adjacent table. Like normal, Horace started up a conversation about the weather and the festival. They all introduced themselves:

"Isiah and I know all about you Shelby, you're the

philanthropic man of the hour who is putting on the festival, what a great effort."

"Well, I have had plenty of help Horace, there are lots of people around here who are aware of the mental and physical strain that the past five years of fire and floods have had on the locals."

"Still, we admire your empathy and commitment," responded Isiah.

Tom got up and offered a shout, it wasn't too difficult to the memory, they were all drinking schooners of the same local Pale Ale. As he walked towards the bar, he saw Sky sitting by herself in the corner. It was obvious she had been crying.

"What's up Sky?"

"It's ok Tom, I just had a nasty customer this afternoon, who wanted a little extra."

"He didn't hurt you, did he? Was he a local?"

"No, a stranger, but I'm fine, I gave him a nosebleed. It's just that sometimes you just want to stop and look at what direction your life is heading."

"You hang-in-there girl, you have an extraordinary talent, and I love our encounters."

She smiled and Tom continued to the bar. It would be another year before this pair realised they had more in common than just massage. Sky would eventually spend it wisely with Tom.

The beers had just been poured when Tom heard a ruckus behind him, he turned to see this bloke abusing Sky, it was a drunk Pimple. Tom flew across the room and shoved the drunk bodily into the wall. Tom figured that this was the unhappy customer. Pimple was no match for this man, whether sober or drunk. He jumped up and shaped up for a fight.

"What's your problem mate?"

"You're my problem, the lady is a friend of mine and it's time you left, boneheads are not wanted here, now beat it!"

Hard heads like Pimple don't go down easy, and his response rubbed Tom the wrong way.

"What lady, she's a whore!"

That earnt him a belly punch, that not only winded the fool, but nearly split his spleen.

"Now beat it before I give you a real hiding, you freak."

Pimple looked up in pain, then smirked a little. Although he was beaten, Pimple's eye flickered with a movement to the left. That told Tom to watch out. Over his right shoulder, a drunk Scrags was about to execute a king-hit. Tom ducked to his right and offered a left-hand uppercut to Scrag's adams-apple. Scotty the bully Banister went down on his knees, gasping for air. Pimple recovered enough to pick up a chair and was about to hit Tom over the head. Suddenly his knees buckled and he crumpled to the floor with the chair. Shelby had heard the ruckus and came to see where his beer was. He offered a simple kick to Pimples crutch that ended the fight.

The bouncer Jake had run over to help, but the incident was over in seconds. He was a friend of Sky as well and thanked Tom and Shelby for their quick action. They helped Jake throw the drunken thugs out the door. Jake's words of wisdom to the sorry Woy Woy lads summed up everyone's thoughts:

"You're not welcome here scumbags, go home, sleep it off, and don't come back!"

Tom went over to check on Sky:

"You handled yourself quite well over there Tom," she said with a smile.

"Just to save you the trouble my dear. Why not come out to the balcony and have a drink with us. I will introduce you to these two fun guys with funny hats and believe me they are gentlemen."

Horace had followed Shelby to the shouting and left Isiah to mind the table. He stood at the door watching the fight, his Judo would be of no help here. The face of the big drunk person who received the thump to the throat was familiar to Horace. He remembered him from the Simon Song encounter in the Nimbin town park and vaguely from the pub in Woy Woy, he was the one trying to chat up Fiona Sharp. He put those thoughts away and started thinking of the fights he had seen in American western movies. Here, there were no broken bottles, window panes, mirrors, and chairs. Nor was there blood and body's lying all over the place. Just two sorry drunks, waddling back to their car in a little pain. Yes, there was one chair on its side, but not broken.

'Americans always exaggerated those cowboy pub fights,' he thought, as he headed back to Isiah with the skirmish news:

"Fights don't last that long in Australia, one and two hit wonders go down with one or two hits. Nothing broken but egos."

A peaceful afternoon followed, it was good company and food. The sun even made a brief appearance through the clouds. It was not a late night and they all looked forward to tomorrow's festival. The crowd was thinning out, so management let Jake off early. He had a shift at the festival in the morning. He had time for one drink, so he bought himself a beer and joined the balcony group. In his change, he received the special messaged coin.

(C...being round, means you roll on without too much friction)

On the way out of the hotel, Horace noticed two limping men, who forgot to book a room. They were making their way to the *'Cannabis Jungle'* shack, to sleep it off, with other rodents.

The next day was still humid, but the rain was holding off. Horace and Isiah were back in the muggy day gear and headed to the festival. Finding a place to park was a problem, the farm was packed with campers. They had to walk some distance. The music just started and got louder the closer they stepped. There was a huge sign over the gates of the Shelby Estate stating, *'She'll be right mate; we are here to help.'* Two burly bouncers reviewed their tickets, one was Jake Carter, he smiled at Horace and Isiah:

"Have a noisy but safe day friends."

Horace acknowledged him; polite manners come easy to some people. Jake had arrived at the festival early to check out the site. Kyle Driver had already set up his *'Deals on Wheels'* truck for sales. Jake was chuffed, he bought a box of mixed vinal records for twenty dollars from his pocket change. *(C...Here I go again).* Jake had recently purchased a player, he always thought records sounded better than CDs.

There were four stages setup around the property, each with varying styles of music, from Blues, Rock, Rap and Country. There were also food trucks, rides for the kids and even an animal farm. It seemed to Horace that Shelby was a smart operator, not only a good bloke to have as a backup in a fight but a great organiser. He hadn't missed the opportunity to raise funds from various quarters. Isiah went to the Blues quadrant, he wanted to hear the Flautist ladies just one more time. Horace said he would find him there later, he wanted to check out the truck deals. He found his way to Kyle Driver's truck and two items got his immediate focus, drink bottles that he thought he recognised:

"They're pretty fancy bottles lad, do you know where they're from."

"I retrieved them from the flooded Wilson River, with a couple of day packs. No identifications."

"I've seen them before, two American tourists had two similar ones when I met them in Western Australia. It was the Hucksters, they were world travellers from Boston and were heading across the Nullarbor on an around Australia journey. The bottles were an anniversary gift from a friend in Africa, he had them especially made in Switzerland."

Kyle just stared at Horace in disbelief:

"Now, that's a crazy coincidence, that recent car accident out of Lismore had two Americans in it, it was probably those Hucksters. There was no identification in the backpacks, I cleaned them up to help with today's charity funds."

"Yes, well I don't think they will be needing them now," said Horace. "It's so sad, they seemed like a nice couple. How much for one of those bottles?"

"You can have the one without the ding in it for ten

bucks. The other one I will just sell with the backpack."

"Thanks that sounds more than fair." Horace had another collectable memory for his vintage school case.

Scrags and Pimple were a little worse for wear, after their hard night. They couldn't sleep it off in the shack, apart from the rats, a group of locals decided to have a bong party. They had to spend a cramped night in the car. In the morning they were not in the mood for the festival. Scrags told his mate to stay in the car while he got the money from Song. They would leave Nimbin with sour thoughts and head south, the treatment here was not what they were expecting.

Jake Carter looked the dishevelled Scrags up and down at the entrance and took his entry fee, with a warning:

"No trouble here today mate, or you get another boot in the butt, do you read me?"

"Yeah, don't get ya knickers in a knot, I'm just picking up something, and I'm leaving this muddy dump."

"Well, that will be doing us all a favour."

Scrags headed for the Blues area and had no trouble finding Simon Song, he stood out like Jesus in his whites, he was standing by the stage. The encounter took a few minutes. Song demanded a receipt. Once the Woy Woy bully boy had the cash in hand, he got Cash-Hope to send a receipt by phone. He gave Song a parting warning and threat:

"Keep up the payments Bozo or our next visit will put you in hospital."

What he didn't know was that Simon Harmony

Song would be doing prison time and be bankrupt in the near future.

On the way back to the car Scrags stopped at Kyle's van to look for any bargains. He saw a quality day backpack. Thinking he could make a profit from it at the Woy Woy pub, he offered Kyle five bucks:

"Price is twenty bucks mate this is a charity day. I washed it clean and dried it, I'll also throw in a drink bottle, with a slight dent in it, that's a bargain."

Debt collectors know how to haggle for a better price. "I'll give ya fifteen."

"No, Eighteen nothing less."

Scrags handed him a twenty and waited for his two-dollar change. Kyle sneered at him with sarcasm.

"Thanks for your charitable contribution, sir, I'm sure you will be rewarded, karma is a bitch."

Scrags, put the coin change into the drink bottle and shook it as a sign of defiance to Kyle, then walked off with a snarl expression thinking that he would get fifty bucks for the pack at the pub. The fancy drink bottle he would keep, to remind him how much he hated Nimbin.

(C…this bloke needs a bath)

Horace met up with Isiah just as the Flautist ladies were finishing their set. He saw the drink bottle and commented on its quality. Horace told him the story of the Hucksters, and Isiah went on a psychologist rant about coincidence and the statistical math behind six degrees of separation. He then touched on the law of diminishing returns, not in relation to economics, but its analogy with the expense of life energies. Horace's attention wandered on this last subject, he wasn't being rude, it was because he heard a song from the country music section that he recognised. It was about a dog named Speed.

The *'The Sultana Bran Flakes'* had the country crowd dancing in the mud by the time Horace and Isiah followed the sound trail. The mood would have picked up after the previous sad ballad. When the groups set ended, Horace had a catch-up chat, and they all agreed to meet for dinner at the Nimbin Pub. The day turned out to be a remarkable success, and the money raised would be welcomed by the flood ravaged victims.

The last night in Nimbin was a lot quieter than the first, there were no cowboy punch-ups. The *'Deals on Wheels'* boys were there and Horace introduced them to *'The Sultana Bran Flakes'*. The whole group took over the back veranda. Right on cue the clouds parted, and a bright smiling sun shone through. The big wet was fading at last. Banshee *'the screaming spirit'* and Dolores, *'the lady of sorrow,'* were just bad memories. The talk was now all about climate change and what's next. Jake Carter walked onto the veranda and into the conversation and offered an answer:

"Well, we have had fire and floods, and we know we can't starve in Australia, so there will be no famine, the only thing I can think of is its time for fun!"

They all drank to that. Kyle and Jake told the group about their encounters with the big boofhead from Woy Woy, and how he left town with his tail between his legs.

Kyle laughed, "I managed to get some money out of the bum for charity, he bought a daypack off me that I found in the river."

At the end of a great night Horace farewelled Chilli

and the lads. They had worked their way south with a couple of gigs and now were heading back to Arnhem Land. Shelby and Tom said their goodbyes and headed back to the farm; they were in for a big clean up the next day. Kyle had a special drop off in Byron Bay before heading back to Coffs. He offered Horace a lift and said he could pick him up in the morning. This suited Isiah, he had to get back to Brisbane for a conference. As they all walked out the front door, they passed these two big men. They appeared to be African and had on suits. In Nimbin they looked totally out of place. They walked straight up to Jake Carter and started asking questions.

CHAPTER 18...BEWARE OF LIONS

In Gaborone, Tebogo Modise and the Larona-pula syndicate were frantic. A month old news bulletin had come through that the Hucksters had been involved in a car accident, one dead, one in a coma. More important to the group, the diamonds were missing. New York contacts in the illegal diamond racket were crying foul. The payment for this consignment of two uncut gems had already been paid into an offshore pending-delivery account. To avoid discovery of criminal money trails, available funds must be visible before processing. These were very special diamonds. After cutting, their value would exceed sixty million dollars.

Tebogo's agents Zahi and Taifa, known as the 'Lions of Mogadishu', were sent to the accident scene. They were a ruthless pair of Somalians who rarely failed on missions around the world. They had orders to recover the special water bottles or face termination. Tebogo's mantra of termination didn't mean from employment either, but he knew this pair always showed 'pride' in their work.

The 'Lions' got to work immediately. They flew into Brisbane, hired a car and headed to Brisbane Hospital to see Clarissa Huckster. They had no luck there, her brother had just transferred her home to Boston. A nurse told them that the police had only retrieved a small bag of female clothes from the accident site. She believed that the bulk of their gear would be still in the wreck. They then headed to Lismore and located the salvaged car wreck at a holding yard just out of town. They thought they were in luck, the car, although full of mud still contained most of the Huckster gear. They found two swiss army knives in leather scabbards in the glove box but nothing else of value. It took a while, and their suits would need dry cleaning from all the river filth. After a thorough search they couldn't find the water bottles. They were also aware that the pair always carried back packs. They were missing as well.

The 'Lions' then checked at the Lismore hospital where Clarissa was first taken, and again no luck. They found out who the onsite emergency crews were and managed to get their contact details. They used a made-up story for sympathy, telling lies about the Hucksters having sponsored children in Botswana. They said they needed important paperwork, photos, and memorabilia from their African Safari to be returned to the children. They were coy about the water bottles and only mentioned the day packs. The locals were all genuine in their responses. Neither the police, paramedics nor tow truck operators had taken anything from the wreckage. All these enquiries came to the notice of Detective Ace Robinson, a local Bundjalung man, who had come up through the police ranks.

The 'Lions' only choice now was to check with local markets. Things were looking grim, two water bottles in a flooded river, the boss would not be happy. They heard about the music festival at Nimbin and thought that with such a large gathering of locals at one venue someone may have heard something, so, they headed for the Nimbin Hotel.

The 'Lions of Mogadishu,' approached Jake Carter in a friendly manner:

"We're after information on a recent local flooding tragedy. A friend of ours drowned in his vehicle, and his family have asked us to help recover some of the equipment lost in the flood. Hotels such as yours have many travellers passing through, and often stories are told. Have you heard anything that could help us?"

Despite their formidable appearance Jake found the pair to be pleasant. So, he responded in a helpful manner. Jake recounted the conversation he had had with Kyle:

"One of the drivers, named Kyle, from the *'Deals on Wheels'* group, who put this festival on, told us that he managed to get some money out of a bloke we threw out of the pub last night. He bought a daypack off him that he had found in the river."

The *'Lions'* interest suddenly peaked, they smiled with pearly whites like a pair of Cheshire cats:

"And who was the bloke you threw out?"

"A drunk from Woy Woy, I heard someone last night say something about them being debt collectors from a mob called Cash-Hope. I remember that because we laughed about them being Cash-no-Hopers. There were two of them, the big ugly boofhead was called Scrags and he called his mate Pimple."

"Weird names?"

"Yep, but somehow suited. That's about all I can help you with, it was a busy night."

"Much appreciated, you have been a major help"

Information on the *'Deals on Wheels'* group was just a google input away. Some sweet talking by Zahi to the office lady was enough to get Kyle Drivers full name and business address in Coffs Harbour, which meant they would be heading in the right direction to Woy Woy as well.

Later that day Jake ran into Shelby in Nimbin and told him about the Africans enquiry.

"They seemed ok mate, but their story was a little bit odd, I mentioned Kyles involvement with the Woy Woy boofheads and these blokes seemed to be over excited when I mentioned the day pack that Kyle sold to the big bloke called Scrags."

"Thanks Jake, I'll give him a call and let him know to expect a visit."

* * *

Hekan Nabbu, a tall Sudanese from the African Crime division of the Australian Federal Police was informed that two Somalian temporary visa holders who had recently come under notice from Interpol, were on the move. Despite the use of burner phones and the dark web, surveillance was still possible on some individuals. Data analysis and grid segmentation of cell phone usage had indicated that these two Somalian Nationals were in the Byron Shire. He had memorandums sent to Police stations in the north to report only if these people were seen.

Ace Robinson the Lismore detective called him the next day and informed him that two large African men were asking questions about a recent car accident and drowning. The Detective filled Hekan in on all the Huckster details, he also said that the Africans were driving a Landcruiser. A picture was now starting to build in his mind. The connection between Botswana, two travelling American tourists and these two Somalian men rang alarm bells of illicit trade. Hekan dispatched Dave Lang, an undercover field agent to the area.

* * *

Kyle dropped Horace off at his motel in Byron Bay. As soon as he put his bags in his roomhe called Waiehu. Isiah had already filled her in on the Nimbin fun and she said he had already notified the Police about the Flautist cults true business, which was drug running. She was enjoying the temporary posting but was looking forward to getting back to Lizard Island.

After the call he wrote his postcards to Fiona and home. He then had to re-pack his old school bag of trinkets which was now nearly full. He picked up the fancy water bottle and studied it. After giving it a thorough clean it came up like new. It was an item of precision manufacture and beauty. The lid was embossed with a transparent plastic type of covering that was embedded with what looked like zircons. For ten dollars he now thought he got a real bargain. It was insulated like a thermos as well and very handy for a nice hot cup of tea. It also appeared to be slightly heavier than it should be. There was a barely visible seal an inch from the bottom that just turned freely in each direction. Horace suspected that it had extra insulation material in the base to give it stability. He placed it in the bag, there was only room now for one more item before he would send it home to the Cotswolds. He still wanted to find a replacement koala piggy bank.

His room at home had shelves of memorabilia from

all his trips. He had one area totally dedicated to his Australian adventures. What Horace didn't know about his latest acquisition was that the bottom section of the bottle was a lock. It needed a combination of turns in both directions to unlock and expose an uncut rare diamond embedded into an opaque bed of silicon. After he settled in, Horace went for a walk around Byron. It was home to the wealthy overseas and local movie stars, plus a mixture of sea changers, government sponsored job seekers and the occasional bogan. Byron's past was not as attractive as it appeared to be today.

Horace woke early and dressed for a warm sunny day. He was back in his cool gear as he called it. This time he left his Derby Bowler in the bag. After lunch he planned to buy another Akubra hat, hire a car, and visit some local attractions. He grabbed a newspaper on his way to breakfast, and the front page headline and story got his attention:

"A psychedelic painted Volks Wagon van was pulled over last night in a Police operation. The drug bust just north of Nimbin made a significant haul of cannabis and about a one hundred thousand dollars in cash, considered the proceeds of crime. The driver, a tall bearded man was accompanied by two women who claimed to be hitch hikers from the recent music festival. They even played their flutes for the police to prove their innocence. They were let go with a warning about the dangers of hitching rides. The driver was charged, and bail refused."

Music to my ears, thought Horace with a laugh, *'those Police lads probably came under the lure of those pretty flautist sirens of charm.'*

Following breakfast, he went for a long beach and

town walk. The beach was packed with tourists. It was one of the best days in weeks, and everybody wanted their fair share of the sun and water. Back on main street he found some upmarket shops that sold name brands with expensive mark-ups. Horace finally found his second Akubra hat in one of those down to Earth surf shops. It was twice the price that he paid in Darwin but he didn't think he would see any more dingos between here and Sydney.

With the new hat in place, protecting his thinning scalp, he made his way to the local watering hole, appropriately called the Beach Hotel, as that's where the best surf beach was situated. There were no real estate agents or funeral directors to talk too so he had a counter lunch and a beer. As he ate and drank, he was reading an article about the town's history. For some 20,000 years the place was known as Cavanbah by the local Bundjalung tribes. European settlers called it that for a while, but in 1894 it was officially changed to Byron Bay. After all, to the English it was an uninhabited country. Post the second world war the town was unkindly described as:

'Reeking from the stench originating from the piggery, meatworks and whaling factories, with their effluent colouring the sea and washing on the shore.'

That reminded Horace of some present-day places in England.

He read that gold was discovered in Byron Bay in the late eighteen hundreds, and the mineral rich beaches were nearly destroyed by the industry. Dairy men started to settle the land as well, which had been cleared by the cedar-getters. Butter production boomed and a cold-storage factory was built next to Byron's railway line.

The Norco company was the ultimate beneficiary. That reminded Horace of the flood victim job losses at the Norco factory in Lismore. He was hoping things would eventually get back to normal.

In the 1930's, he read that the first meatworks opened. The smell from the meat and dairy works was appalling, and the annual slaughter of migrating whales made matters worse. The long board surfers came in the sixties as the smells faded. Then the body odour smells of peace and free love came back with the Hippies in the seventies. They called it a groovy happening. Around this time, a television comedian, acquired a rundown pub opposite Byron Bay's main beach. Following an extensive renovation, it would become the watering hole known as Beachys.

Byron Bay today is one of the most up-market residential areas on the Australian east coast. With its alternative new-age shops, spiritual services, meditation, yoga classes, holistic healing and wellness retreats. Horace felt brain shocked with detail and headed for Cape Byron and its famous light house. It is the eastern most point of the Australian mainland. Cook named it after a Captain John Byron, another chap who liked to sail around the world. For one hundred years feral goats from shipwrecks occupied the precarious cliffs that surrounded the lighthouse. A few people commented to Horace that some of the locals are human feral-goats, but wealth seemed to be the mainstay. The Byron area didn't suit Horace, he preferred more unspoilt places so he only stayed one more night then headed south to Coffs Harbour.

* * *

Dave Lang stopped to refill at a petrol station just off the freeway near Ballina when he spotted two large African males in a Landcruiser, they were heading south in a hurry. He took a gamble that they were his objective and changed plans. He headed south back towards Coffs Harbour. Our intrepid travel writer Horace was only about three cars behind; he planned a night at a motel near the Surf Club at Park Beach. He was told the Club food was great, as was the ocean view. He had two objectives the next day, a visit to Mutton Bird Island, then onto Nambucca Heads to see why so many of his English friends like the place.

The following morning was clear and warm. Horace had breakfast at the Surf Club then drove to the Coffs marina. Mutton Bird Island was connected to the mainland by an easy walking spit of land. It is the home to thousands of wedge-tailed shearwaters, so called for their ability to cut or shear the water with their wings as they skim across the surface. Early settlers called them mutton birds because of their fatty mutton or sheep like flesh. Horace enjoyed the walk and on the way back chatted to some fishermen unloading a huge catch. Horace noticed that many Australians just love what they do for a living. These lads were laughing and singing as they worked. It was addictive, and it put a spring in his step as he headed back to the car.

Just north of Nambucca, Horace turned off the expressway to have a look at Valla Beach. What a surprise. In England there are few places you can go and not see people. Horace went down to a creek crossing, near one of those senior retirement resorts. There was this footbridge that crossed the creek. It looked like it was built by the Flintstones, but it was sturdy. On the other side of the bridge he walked over a sand dune and discovered the vast expanse of the Pacific Ocean. It was a ten-kilometre beach and Nambucca was in the distance. What startled Horace the most was that there wasn't another person anywhere on that stretch of pristine sand. At that moment he was thinking how Australians are spoilt with land and resources. His next stop was the V-Wall Hotel at Nambucca Heads for lunch.

What a magic place Nambucca turned out to be. The delta of this river settlement seemed vast. There were unspoilt views to the south of beaches, sand dunes and river channels. The walk out to the headland was time travelling with human expressions. All the large rocks that made up the seawall were covered with coloured art and the thoughts of visitors from all over the world. Some may call it sanctioned graffiti, but to Horace it was an open-air gallery of life. To add to his delight, once again there were dolphins riding the river currents out to sea.

Dave Lang drove around Coffs Harbour hoping to find the Africans in their Landcruiser, but to no avail. He checked with Hekan for updates and the only leads were some suspect cell activities around Taree. They were running out of clues, but these Africans were now definitely heading south. Hekan said he would get back in touch after talking to the Lismore Detective again. Dave decided to stop for a lunch break at the V-Wall Hotel in Nambucca Heads. The place had only a few patrons when he walked up to the bar. There was a strange fella ordering a drink. He was talking to the barman with a strong English accent but was dressed like a 'Crocodile Dundee' enthusiast, with a freshly drycleaned outfit and a brand-new Akubra hat. Like always Horace couldn't resist a communication challenge:

"How are you lad, my names Horace, are you enjoying a bit of sunshine at last?"

"Yes, you can call me Dave, you are spot on, the rain has been a constant pain of late. I can tell by the accent your English, are you on a tour?"

"Yes, you could say that, but it's more like a working and learning experience. I'm on the final leg now, I have been circumnavigating your wonderful country, meeting many people and having great adventures. What about yourself?"

"It's all work for me, I was heading to Lismore to investigate a problem, and just now got turned around to head south again."

"That sounds intriguing, what do you do for a living?"

"I would have to terminate you if I told you that," Dave laughed. "You could say I'm on a mission of good will. Tell me about your adventures Horace."

"You would need a week to hear it, I'm a travel writer, so one day it will be in my employer's 'Finding Earth Magazine.' Recently I've been to a music festival in Nimbin, and beach villages from Byron Bay to here."

"I will keep a look out for the publication. Nimbin you say, I bet that was an eye opener for you?"

"Certainly was, punch ups with bogans from Woy Woy in the pub, drug running cults of flute playing ladies, and music loving Byron Bay Hippies. All great fodder for my readers."

"Did you hear about those Americans caught in the floods up that way?"

"Not only heard about them, but I also met them, in

Western Australia."

Dave nearly choked on his beer; he couldn't believe his luck. At last, a clue. Horace went on to tell Dave all he knew about his brief encounter with the Hucksters. Their mention of an African safari, and their around Australia plans. Then the coincidence of talking to Kyle Driver, who had found two back packs downstream from an accident of people Horace had met thousands of kilometres away. He didn't mention the water bottle he bought. He was a bit embarrassed about buying an item that belonged to someone he knew who recently died. Dave couldn't hide his excitement:

"Did you see or hear of anyone asking questions about the Hucksters and their African trip?"

"No, but when we were leaving the pub on the night after the festival, two large African men in suits, who seemed out of place, went in to talk to Jake Carter the bouncer. What is the story here Dave? Are they looking for something? Are you a law enforcement officer?"

"Yes, I'm involved in field enquiries and you have been an immense help, but that's all I can say, ok. It sounds like the Hucksters may have been couriers of something. These Africans are known to my employers and they seem extremely interested in the luggage."

"Well, I can tell you where some of the luggage went. Those bogans in the pub fight were from Woy Woy. They were debt collectors from a mob called Cash-Hope. They were in town to get some arrears from a bloke called Simon Song who was thought to be a cult leader. Turns out he was a drug runner. The Police pulled him over a few days ago. The story was on the radio. The Woy Woy lads had strange tags, the big bully bloke was Scrags and his weedy mate was called Pimple. They were unwelcome visitors with attitude. They got thrown out of the pub by two *'Deals on Wheels'* drivers and the bouncer Jake."

"Thanks, Horace you have been a major help. I will give you my number, could you please ring if you think of anything more. I must fly, looks like I'm off to Woy Woy. Can I have your contact details?"

"No problem Dave, glad to do my bit. Please let me know how you go; I can see a good story in this."

* * *

Kyle had received a call from Shelby and informed him that Jake Carter had told him about the two Africans making enquiries about the Hucksters accident. Shelby said that they had rung the office girl as well and they now had the Coffs address:

"I'm just a bit concerned that these blokes were very keen on details when they questioned Jake. Although Jake told me they were courteous, he thought they were a bit aggressive and their story was a little suspect. I also called Ace Robinson in Lismore, that detective we met on that golf weekend, he seems to know something about these Africans. Just be wary mate."

Kyle was a lean man and not a mean man. Like all Shelby's franchise owners, he had a *'she'll be right'* attitude. It was what his wife Linda loved about him. Linda was a nurse and on shift when Kyle heard the knock on the door.

The *'Lions of Mogadishu'* had a stroke of luck when driving past the Big Banana at Coffs Harbour. They spotted a yellow *'Deals on Wheels'* van parked in a side street. It wasn't Kyles business address it was his home. When Kyle answered the door he stood back, a bit stunned at the size of these brutes, but the 'Lions' were at first friendly. They gave the same story about the children in Botswana and the need to recover some items. Kyle told them all about the recovery of day packs from the river when they suddenly became a little more aggressive:

"Yes, that's good, but were there any water bottles in the packs?"

Kyle then realised that there was more to this recovery mission. He didn't want to end up as a wall trophy in a safari hut, so told them everything he could think of in relation to the packs. He held back on one item. He didn't mention the water bottle he sold to Horace; he didn't want these clowns harassing an Englishman who he liked. Kyle told them he only found one bottle with a ding in it and two muddy day packs full of wet weather gear. He sold the wet weather gear and one day pack that he had cleaned up to various unknown people on the day. The other pack and water bottle he sold to that Woy Woy bloke called Scrags:

"Are you sure there was only one bottle? They were special items and the Botswana kids need them back as a memorial to their American friends."

"Yes, that's my full recollection of the sales." Kyle was thinking this story of theirs was total bull-shite.

As he spoke, they stared at him with killer eyes, they were hunting for lies. There was silence for a few minutes as they watched him. Then suddenly in a blind flash, a huge fist knocked Kyle out cold. The 'Lions of Mogadishu,' had a fresh gazelle, they hog tied and gagged him then threw Kyle into the back of the Landcruiser with a canvas tarp as covering. Their prey would come in handy when they confronted the Woy Woy boofheads. Before they left the house, they found keys to Kyle's truck and parked it in a warehouse area with many factories for lease signs. Kyle's wife will think he is on another drop off somewhere and that would buy the 'Lions' some more time.

CHAPTER 19...SIX DEGREES OF TROUBLE

A week after arriving home from Nimbin, Cash-Hope had left a message for another job at Port Stephens for Scrags. This time Pimple wasn't invited. Scrags was about to kick his mate out of the shack. After the trouble in Nimbin, they had not been talking. Scrags blamed Pimple for all the trouble, because of the massage he had. He decided to give his mate the boot when he returned from Nelson Bay.

Pimple knew his pending eviction was coming. He knew Reeya should be back from Greece by now because she had sent him a post card from her last night in Athens. She wrote it would be good to catch up sometime. Pimple was thinking this might be a chance to get out of Woy Woy and start a new life. When Scrags left, he started to pack. He didn't own much, but he had a little cash from the sale of his last crop of weed. He looked around the shack for anything of value. Under Scrag's bed he found a half bottle of Johnny Walker Blue and the Nimbin day pack. The fancy water bottle was in the pack. He poured the whisky into the water bottle for something to drink on the train to Sydney.

The only thing Pimple left behind were unpaid house bills on which he scribbled:

'Thanks for nothing scumbag.'

He stopped in to say goodbye to his mum, but she was drunk and well on the way to passing out. He cursed the wasted time and left a note on the sideboard saying that he was visiting his girlfriend Reeya Lambros in Winston Street, North Sydney.

* * *

Horace took two days to get to Nelson Bay after leaving Nambucca. He stopped at the Trial Bay Gaol at South West Rocks. Prisoners of war stories, and the convict labours of his homeland's tyranny always fascinated him. He spent a night at a nineteenth century pub on the Hastings River at Port Macquarie and watched dolphins riding waves at the town beach. He chatted to a real estate agent in the pub and told him all about dolphin mating habits. After that memory brag he went back to his room and rang Waiehu. He told her all about talking to Dave Lang and the connection to the Hucksters from his time in Walpole. Every time he spoke with Waiehu his admiration grew. He was now thinking what fun it would be to lay with her on a sandy beach in the sun on Lizard Island.

He arrived at Nelson Bay just around lunch time and drove up the hill to the Light House at Little Beach. A friend had told him that it's the best place to see the headland adjacent to Shoal Bay. As he approached the old Light House he was suddenly taken in by the view. This place was truly a wonderland. Two magnificent mountain peaks guarding the harbour's entrance added to the magic. Together with these mountain peaks, the crystal blue bay of water lapping onto a white sandy beach was a stunning vista. Horace had been to many beautiful places around the world, and this place was up there with the best of them.

Horace entered the museum on site and learnt about the area's Aboriginal and Military history. The local Worimi Tribe had named these volcanic plug mountains Tomaree and Yaccaba. They had inhabited the Port Stephens area for thousands of years before the English ships arrived. Horace decided to have lunch there, and the café had only a few people in it. He sat for an hour eating and chatting to the waitress, while Lorikeets, Noisy miners and Magpies fought over scraps of food. The waitress told him of some of the interesting places to visit while at the Bay. Two things grabbed his attention, the walk up Tomaree Mountain to the 360-degree viewing platform and the Birubi Beach sand-dunes camel and adventure rides. He already had his camel ride experience in Broome but the 4WD dune ride sounded like great fun. On the way out of the cafe he entered the gift shop, the first thing he laid eyes on was a koala piggy bank. It had a sticker on it saying:

'Koalas were once plentiful around Port Stephens, we now need to protect them'.

This wonderful item and reminder of this beautiful place will just fit into the old school case.

'I'll post the lot home tomorrow,' he thought, as he headed back to the car.

Horace had pre-booked for a two-night stay at the Shoal Bay Hotel. After settling into his room he met the challenge of walking up Tomaree Mountain. It was a hard slog, but the waitress was right, the view was worth it. Back at the pub Horace had a well earned beer and whiled away the afternoon catching up on his notes. He booked the 4WD dune ride for the next day and had an early night, dreaming about being chased by dingoes over sand dunes.

* * *

The 'Lions of Mogadishu,' rang Cash-Hope and asked to speak with the gentleman debt collector named Scrags from Woy Woy. The girl who answered laughed:

"Scrags, what planet are you from, Scotty Bannister is no gentleman. He only works for us occasionally, and his on his way to Anna Bay for a collection as we speak."

The lady wouldn't give too many details over the phone, but Zahi gave a story about catching up with his old mate Scrags, and as he was travelling back to Sydney now, it would be a good opportunity. All she would give him was the street in Anna Bay, no number and the time he left Woy Woy in their car. That was enough, the 'Lions' worked the travel time out, they would get there before him to watch the street.

When they arrived at Anna Bay, they stopped at a hardware store and bought two cream buckets and a shovel. They then watered their captive Kyle and gave him a knock-out syringe of 'Liquid Ecstasy', he was out cold in seconds. The Africans then waited at the head of the street. They wanted to interrogate these guys together. Thirty minutes later a ute with a Cash-Hope logo on the side came into the street. A big bloke jumped out of the ute in a driveway a few doors down and bashed on the door.

"This is our man, Zahi. Let him conduct his business first, and when he comes out, we will grab him. There is no one around."

It didn't take Scrags long to get the money that was

owing. In ten minutes he came out shovelling some cash into his pocket. The two Africans were waiting at the ute as Scrags approached. A glock pistol, held by Taifa was aimed at his head:

"What's this about?"

"Just shut your mouth and put your hands behind your back, you'll find out later."

Scrags could see that these blokes were serious, the only resistance he showed was a mouthful of expletives and a racist slur. The 'Lions' hated this bloke instantly. Scrags put his hands behind his back and Zahi cable tied them tight enough to draw blood. The Woy Woy bully yelped in pain. In that instant Taifa injected a syringe into Scrag's neck. It happened so fast he was in total surprise and went limp in seconds. They gagged him and jointly threw him under the tarp with Kyle. The whole exercise was over in a few minutes and there were no witnesses visible. Both captives will wake up, looking at each other's heads and realise their buried up to their necks in sand.

* * *

Horace was up early in the morning; he was booked in for the Birubi Beach 4WD dune ride around eleven. He dressed once more in his khaki adventure outfit and with the Akubra hat on, he thought he looked like he was ready for a real desert sand dune safari. After breakfast the first job was to post the now full school case back home. His Mum would place all the items on the Australian shelves and look forward to hearing the stories that surrounded them when Horace returned home. The Post Office at Nelson Bay was quiet, and there were no problems with the priority paid air mail. *'Finding Earth Magazine'* allowed for expensive deliveries like this in their contracts, and his mum knew it was on its way.

On the way to Birubi Beach Horace drove through Anna Bay, it was a quiet little village. As he passed the local hardware store, two familiar faces walked out carrying some buckets and a shovel. They were the Africans from Nimbin. Horace pulled the car over and rang Dave Lang.

A lot had happened since Horace last spoke with Dave. A search was on for the *'Deals on Wheels'* driver Kyle. His wife had rung Shelby about her missing husband. Shelby arranged with his detective friend Ace in Lismore to organise a search. That detective was in communication with Hekan Nabbu. Then Kyles truck was found abandoned in a Coffs business yard. All pieces fell together. Hekan used all the new knowledge and went through the same lady at Cash-Hope that the Africans had rung. Dave was directed to Anna Bay and was almost there when Horace rang.

❋ ❋ ❋

The sand dunes of Stockton beach seemed to go on forever. It was not unlike the Sahara Desert. The *'Lions of Mogadishu'* were parked in a secluded spot, and their trail was barely noticeable amongst the other four-wheel drive tracks in this desert landscape. They dragged their hapless hostages to a location surrounded by high sand dunes, where there were no tracks. Zahi and Taifa dug the pits by hand and shovel with ease in the soft sand. They bound the feet of the still unconscious Scrags and Kyle, then buried them up to their necks.

Kyle was the first to awake, there was a dreadful smell of urine. He opened his eyes and was looking at the head of the bloke he had sold the pack and bottle to, there was a liquid dripping off his face. The Africans, who were sitting cross legged adjacent to him had obviously relieved themself. While Zahi sat there sharpening a large Bowie knife Taifa was first to talk, he had a soft educated voice:

"You can see by the position you have found yourself in that we are determined to find out the truth. We wish to know the location of the back packs and their contents that you sold to this racist pig whose head is before you. Speak truthfully, and you will not die by our hand."

Kyle was dehydrated and groggy but tried to explain:

"I have told you all I know."

"Quiet!" Spoke Zahi, "we will wait, when the racist awakes, we wish to see his reaction to your answers."

Kyle asked for water and Taifa splashed a few drops on his tongue. There was silence for two minutes and then Scrags began to stir. His eyes opened and a moment later a mouth full of hate and threats lashed out at the Africans. Once again Taifa responded:

"You are in no position to be causing us any threats Mr Racist, we want you to answer some questions, shortly, but first we want you to listen to what your compatriot here has to say. Is that understood?"

"You two black bast......" That was as far as Scrags temper lasted, Zahi slashed his cheek with the knife and blood flowed into the sand. The Woy Woy bully squealed as the blood and urine mixed, and he went silent.

"Now we have his attention tell us your story Mr Kyle."

Kyle reiterated the same story he said originally:

"I only found one bottle with a ding in it and two muddy day packs full of wet weather gear. I sold the wet weather gear and one day pack, that I had cleaned up to various unknown people on the day. The other pack and water bottle I sold to this bloke Scrags, who argued over a lousy two bucks."

As he spoke the Africans watched both heads closely. Then Scrags spoke with mumbled pain filled words, he had calmed his aggression:

"I don't know what your problem is, that's all there is to it. If you want the stuff, I bought off this bloke, all you had to do was ask for it."

Taifa, turned to Kyle and thanked him. Then gagged him again and placed a bucket over his head. Knowing what his question would be if he allowed Kyle to talk, he answered:

"Yes, as I said, you will not die by our hand, we will let nature take its course."

They then turned back to Scrags, Zahi held the knife point on the other cheek, and with the eyes of a hunter who would skin an elephant asked:

"And where exactly will we find the goods Mr Racist."

This time Scrags was thinking of his survival, if they left him like Kyle, there was a chance to live. He told them his address, the bag and bottle were under the bed, and that his mate Pimple would be there to assist. They believed him. Zahi slashed his other cheek and Taifa

HORACE AND THE COIN

kicked him in the head, with the words:

"I hate stingy racist bullies."

They both laughed and placed the other bucket on his head. Debt collector Scotty Banister had found his karma at last. The 'Lions of Mogadishu' kicked some more sand up on the buckets and headed off to Woy Woy with cheesy grins and no remorse.

Dave told Horace he had just received a call from the Lismore detective Ace Robinson, and he and Kyles mate Shelby had come down here to Anna Bay to help find their friend. We can all meet at the Birubi Beach Surf Club café in the next half hour:

"The local police have also been notified, and I gave them the details of the buckets and shovel you told me about. They believe that these African blokes are heading into the sand dunes. The police are also placing a roadblock on Nelson Bay Road, there is only one road into this place and two Africans in a Landcruiser should be easy to find. Do you want to help with the search Horace? I have no problem, the more eyes the better."

"Thanks Dave, I would be happy to help in finding the lad, I just hope he is ok."

"Well, we will do our best, this detective Ace has some Aboriginal tracking skills. The Police will come in from the north near Bobs Farm. We will approach from the surf club. With some luck we will find your friend. I rang ahead and the 4WD dune safari group were very helpful, they will provide four units with drivers and walky-talkies to help in the search."

The 'Lions of Mogadishu' were not nervous fools, they had a police scanner and heard that a roadblock was in operation. They had evaded many such problems in the past. They drove back to Nelson Bay and dumped the car in a Woolworths car park. They then walked to the marina and hopped onto the ferry to Tea Gardens. They blended in with many other multinational tourists and enjoyed the adventure, they even saw a dolphin. When they arrived at Tea Gardens, they surveyed the streets and found a business property with many cars. One car, an older model sedan had bird droppings on the roof and cobwebs on the handles. It obviously had not been used for a while. They broke in, hotwired it, and had it running in seconds. It even had a full tank of fuel. They then headed off to Woy Woy.

✳ ✳ ✳

The four search groups gathered at the surf club and planned their routes. Within an hour they had travelled all the main tracks. Ace then called up and said that there were some fresh tracks just west of his present location. He and the driver followed them to a point where they stopped, close to a series of high sand dunes. The good news was, there were a few footprints and drag marks. The whole group then headed to that location. They all spread out and each climbed a sand dune. Horace struggled up his, and when he reached the top, he was on all fours. In the shadow of the next dune over, there were two barely visible sandy lumps. They were a creamy colour, and a slightly different shade to the sand, one even had a red tinge around it. He stood and shouted to the others.

Shelby was first on site and lifted the bucket, it was Scrags and he was well and truly expired. He grabbed the other bucket and Kyle moved his head. Shelby yelled out

'*He's alive!*' and removed the gag. Kyle took a deep breath and passed out. He came around in the ambulance, Shelby was with him, and the paramedic smiled with the words:

"He's a survivor mate."

He gave him some water; the saline drip did the rest. Kyle's first words were:

"I know where their heading...Woy Woy."

Shelby rang Kyles wife Linda with the good news and then Dave Lang with that location information. He then turned back to Kyle, held his hand, and said:

"She'll be right mate, ... Linda knows you survived and will be coming home soon."

CHAPTER 20...SIX DEGREE SEPARATION

(C...cryptic title, I know)

Zahi and Taifa were feeling lucky, they had avoided the police. They drove straight to Scrag's shack in Smith Street Blackwall. They were in and out well before the police got organised. There were always delays when two or more agencies were involved. The *'Lions'* had no need to break in, Pimple had left the front door unlocked. There was no sign of him. They searched the whole house and found nothing. Their anger was growing, but they found some paperwork in a kitchen draw with a couple of clues. A post card from Greece to Peter Simple from some woman called Reeya, it just stated that they should catch up sometime.

"Not really a love letter." Laughed Zahi.

The other piece was of more value, it was a bill addressed to a Mrs. Simple. It had a note on it that asked Peter to pay it. Mrs. Simple lived only two streets away. When they arrived, she was asleep on the front porch and virtually unconscious, with a half empty flagon of wine at her feet. They walked straight past her into the house. A brief search revealed the note Peter left with Reeya's Winston Street address in North Sydney. They kept all the information they found so the police trail would go cold and then walked out passed the drunk lady who never even stirred. By the time the police arrived at Smith Street the Africans were on the freeway to Sydney.

The 'Lions' had called another Australian based Larona-
pula agent. It was their brother Axmed. He arranged the
hire. Axmed had driven across the continent to evade
the West Australian agency wide investigation into the
Trussell stabbing. He was looking forward to a catch up
with his brothers soon. Zahi and Taifa had dumped the
Tea Gardens car in a supermarket and picked up a new
hire car in Gosford.

The Woy Woy police tried to notify family and hotel
friends of Scott Bannister's death, to no avail and no one
came forward. Cash-Hope were then notified about the
death of their employee, but they were only interested in
the cash he had received and wanted nothing to do with
a burial. Eventually the police would use the cash they
found in his pocket to help with the burial costs. His life
went by with no reflection and forgotten in a pauper's
grave.

Dave Lang was sure the police in Woy Woy would
get the Africans, now they had the address. After the
incident Dave, Horace, and Ace went back to the Bay Hotel
to celebrate the success of finding Kyle.

Dave raised his schooner:

"A toast gentleman to a successful adventure, a
triumph, and a well organised plan of attack."

Horace with a Shakespearian smirk quoted:

'That which we call a rose by any other name would
smell as sweet.' "A good man has been saved."

Ace just looked on bemused, then Dave's phone
rang. The police were too late, the Africans had fled
and the trail had gone cold in Woy Woy. A brief time
later another call came through. Hekan Nabbu informed
Dave that a phone message intercept had indicated the

Africans may be heading back to Sydney. Horace saw a lift opportunity:

"Any chance of a lift tomorrow mate? If I can drop this car off in Newcastle, it will save a lot of run arounds in Sydney's nightmare traffic. I was heading back tomorrow to Kirribilli for a show, I have tickets and a B&B booked in Milson Point."

"Not a problem Horace, I'll drop you off there."

They thanked Ace for his help, he was heading back to Lismore and they picked up their gear from the hotel. Horace had one last look at the beautiful Shoal Bay headland, and they hit the road to Sydney.

❉ ❉ ❉

Pimple arrived at Milson Point station and drank the last swig of whiskey. He nearly choked on the coin, which washed into his mouth. *(C...awake at last... hic!)* He spat the coin onto his hand and saw the inscription:

'And that's just what I'll do, finally spend something wisely.'

With that thought he put the coin in his top pocket and walked to Reeya's town house. When he knocked on the door, the response was not what he expected:

"What are you doing here?"

"I came to catch up, like you said in the post card, I've moved on from Woy Woy and thought I would give our relationship a leg up."

Reeya just stared at him, she had moved on and met a new man in Greece. The post card was meant to be a brush off, but this thick idiot took it the wrong way:

"It's like this Peter, I met someone new while in Athens. He is a real gentleman with a life plan. It's what I need. I'm sorry you got the wrong impression, good luck in the future."

Pimple was in shock, the words 'wrong impression', and 'good luck' were floating in his brain like daggers of rejection. His weaknesses erupted in fury and he shoved Reeya backwards into the house. She laid on the carpet crying, he was having thoughts of forcing her into submission when her father came down the stairs. Peter saw him coming, slammed the front door and fled down the street with a torn heart screaming, "die bitch!"

Mr Lambros helped his daughter up, she wasn't hurt. He then rang the police about the assault and gave a description and name of the attacker. The words Peter Simple and Woy Woy bought immediate attention to a current person warrant issued at Port Stephens. Which then came to the attention of Dave Lang, he now had a North Sydney address to go to.

Pimple was between worlds; he didn't know what to do, he was depressed to the point of self-harm. He had a cousin who lived in a one-bedroom social housing flat in the Greenway building in Kirribilli. He thought maybe Albert would put him up for the night. Albert wasn't exactly happy to see him, he had an early morning shift at a local nursing home. He relented after some persuasion and told Pimple he could sleep on the lounge, one night only and leave at the same time as him in the morning. That was better than sleeping rough, so Pimple agreed. The next morning he was walking the streets of North Sydney. He knew his funds would run out fast, but he couldn't move back in with Scrags, so it looked like he would have to head back to his mum's place. That thought didn't make him happy. He headed for a pub, thinking to wash away his mood before catching a late train back to Woy Woy.

* * *

After Dave Lang dropped Horace off at the Milson Point B&B, he went to interview Reeya Lambros. She told him that Peter had a misunderstanding of their relationship and came to Sydney thinking that they would be an item. Dave listened to her story and told her how lucky she was not to get involved. From recent discussions he had with people who had met this bloke he was a real loser. Reeya, didn't comment, she was embarrassed by the incident. She was of no help with the location of Pimple either, but she could remember him telling her once that he had a cousin near her home. That was useful info, Dave was thinking:

'great, maybe he was still around'.

He rang Horace to keep an eye out for Pimple, and that he would be around the area for a few days, if he wanted to meet for a beer. He also brought him up to speed on the Reeya connection. Horace had settled into the B&B then went for a walk and found a nice Milson Point café for an evening coffee.

Unknown to Marcus Canning was all the drama that was taking place in his area. He had walked from his Tree House Café in Lavender Bay Road to Fiona Sharpe's pre prison address. The Landlord of the premise was sent an evidence item which was no longer required from *'The Bobbitt of Lavender Bay'* case. It was a razor-sharp

Samurai sword. The Landlord was thinking of keeping it but changed his mind when he heard about its history. He had received Marcus's contact details from the police and rang him to come and collect it. Although it had some bad and painful experiences attached to it, Sally insisted he get it as a reminder to always be faithful.

The twilight was ending, it would be a dark moonless night and Horace was just finishing his coffee. He was about to head back to the B&B when all the excitement happened. First the weedy guy who was called Pimple walked past. Horace was about to call Dave Lang when a Landcruiser pulled up and the two Africans jumped out and grabbed Pimple.

(C...alas poor Pimple, I knew him well. The coin falling out of his shirt pocket, with the message of spending love wisely, was of no use to him now)

They dragged him into the alley. Shortly afterwards, Marcus Canning walked out of the side street, his head was down like his mind was elsewhere. He bent down to pick up a coin near the alley and continued walking past the shops. Horace had never met Marcus but he was good with faces and remembered his picture at the Tree House Café when he met Sally. What got his attention was the samurai sword he was carrying.

Dave Lang had decided to drive around the streets of the area in the hope of spotting Pimple. That's when he saw the Africans. He called for backup and followed them. David pulled up at the café and ran with his gun drawn into the alley. Horace rang the police and all hell broke out with flashes of gunfire and shouting. Then one of the Africans ran out and drove off in the Landcruiser.

Taifa had pulled out his Bowie knife and stabbed

Pimple in the heart for all the trouble he had caused them. When Dave had entered the alley he yelled out 'stop', but it was too late for Pimple. He fired, and Taifa went down, he was momentarily stunned. The bullet passed through his left cheek and took some teeth with it. Zahi thought his brother had been killed when Dave Lang fired. He saw an opportunity grabbed the backpack and bottle. He shoved Dave into the wall and fled the alley. Dave got to his feet and fired at the retreating African but missed. Zahi drove off. Dave was thinking at least he had killed one of the beasts and turned back to check on Pimple. The scrawny kid from Woy Woy was dead, with the knife still in his chest. Taifa didn't have time to remove it. Dave was on his knees when the African regained his senses. He stood up and shoved the agent out of the way and ran. Dave got to his feet and chased after him.

It was getting very dark when Horace nervously walked from the café towards the alley. He saw the two men run out, the large African was holding his cheek and Dave was chasing him. Horace yelled out to Dave that he had called the Police. He went into the alley and the lad Pimple was there with a Bowie knife in his chest. This poor chap would end up buried in a pauper's grave next to his old mate. His mother would sober up for the occasion and cry, before retiring home to a personal wake, and another flagon. Horace stood there thinking that a Shakespearian drama had nothing on this tragedy, and he couldn't think of one funny line. Then he thought of Pimples unrequited desire for Reeya, and a quote popped into his head:

'The stroke of death is as a lovers pinch, which hurts and is desired.'

Dave chased Taifa through the Milson Point station

then down Lavender Bay Road. Blood was running down Taifa's cheek and on to his shirt, he was starting to feel faint from exertion and blood loss. He started to slow down a little around the time he caught up with Marcus, on his way home. Taifa saw the sword grabbed it and pushed Marcus out of the way. He released the scabbard and turned to face Dave. The big African launched with the razor-sharp sword. Dave was caught short; his gun was still holstered. He raised his left arm, it took the full force of the blow, it was a deep cut, but didn't sever his arm. Dave went to the ground bleeding profusely. He braced himself for another blow from the enraged African when a gunshot echoed from across the road.

Hekan Nabbu arrived on site just in time, Taifa laid dead in the gutter with a bullet in the brain. Marcus applied a tourniquet to stop Dave bleeding to death and Hekan rang for the Ambulance. The Samurai sword would not be hanging in Marcus Cannings trophy room that night, once again it was required for evidence.

The next day Horace visited Dave in hospital. They had managed to save his arm but he would be off work for a while. They talked about the incident, and it was great therapy for both. That night he rang Waiehu, she was dining with the Couches. It was all over the news and even Horace was interviewed by the media. He gave Waiehu the full story in detail. Isiah jumped on the phone and offered Horace some of his trauma psychology which he listened to with grace. Horace then told Waiehu that he had a few things to tidy up in Sydney and then he could fly back to Brisbane for a visit before going home if she wished. She was over the moon; she had missed him as much as he had her.

That night Horace had well-wisher calls from all

over. His mum rang him first, that was followed by Mozzy, Walter Shakeshaft, Doug Pitt, and Plane Bob. It seemed to Horace that his list of friends was growing fast.

When Marcus arrived back at the café he sat with Sally and talked about the incident. He reached into his pocket when he remembered picking up the coin, and sat there in stunned silence:

"What's wrong Marcus?"

"This coin, I had it engraved for you prior to my indiscretion. Last night I picked it up on the footpath at Milson Point. What are the chances? it must be an omen."

The coin had finished its journey around Australia and finally found its way back to Marcus. He had a gold chain fitted by Jacks key cutting business next door. That week he approached Sally in the café and went down on one knee. With heart felt sorrow he placed the chain around her neck with the words:

"Love is a currency, from now on Sally I intend to spend it wisely."

(C...I'm home at last, and comfortable, but hang in there because Horace's troubles aren't over yet)

CHAPTER 21...SIX DEGREES OF ANGLES

In Sydney Horace needed a couple of days rest. It had been a frantic adventure down the east coast. He had an interview with Hekan Nabbu to outline his story of events. To Horace's disappointment they still had no idea on what the Africans were after. They did have suspicions that the Hucksters may have been transporting some illegal product through Australia as a ruse to evade suspicion. He concluded it may have been something to do with Botswana's illegal diamond trade but said no more. He thanked Horace for his help and wished him well.

Horace returned to his B&B and finished off his notes. It had been a great learning experience and the articles he was preparing for the *'Finding Earth Magazine'* would make his boss happy. He wrote one last postcard to Fiona and wished her well. He was not prepared to visit her in prison. The last thing he needed was for her to form an attraction to him and perhaps stalk him when she was released. That funny thought led him to remember his promise to Trevor Trussell to try and find Susan.

(C...Fiona was paroled for good behaviour twelve months later. While in prison she formed a relationship with a guard, lucky for him he didn't collect swords and he was faithfull)

Gladys was probably out having a swim when Horace rang. He left a message if she had any idea what

Susan's maiden name was and asked if she could ring him back with any details. The next day he decided to visit the *'Tree House Café'*, it was time to meet the *'Bobbitt of Lavender Bay'*.

Horace rang first thing in the morning and Marcus and Sally were both there. He dressed in his usual business attire and walked down the road to the café. There was still police tape around the scene of the sword attack and blood was still on the pavement. It was a gruesome memory. The Cannings welcomed him on his arrival, Sally remembered him from when he purchased the koala piggy bank. The bowler hat always helped with people's memories. Horace noticed the coin on the chain around her neck:

(C...He took his time to notice me, I only followed him around Australia)

She told Horace the story of how Marcus had it etched with some wisdom words of love and how it was lost and then found again:

"The coin that is," she laughed, "I've always loved my man."

Marcus was still in a bit of shock over the sword incident. He had seen Horace on the television talking about the incident and was keen to hear more of his story. They spoke for an hour, and only briefly touched on the Fiona Sharpe saga. He told them about Trevor Trussell's murder and his need to locate his wife Susan in Sydney. In a strange twist of fate, at that moment, his phone rang, it was Gladys. She had found an old unsent letter in a box under the guest room bed. It was addressed to Harry and Ruth Canning in Parramatta.

Horace listened to what Gladys had to say and

thanked her for her help. He had a look of amazement on his face when he turned to face Sally and Marcus:

"You wouldn't by chance know a Susan Canning, would you?"

"Yes, that's my sister why?"

"Did she ever live in Western Australia, and are your parents Harry and Ruth?"

"Yes, she just returned after being missing for years."

"Well, there is a chance, that I have found Trevor Trussell's wife."

Marcus rang his parent's home straight away.

Susan never mentioned anything of her Western Australian past to her parents or Marcus when they had a reunion party. She was now living in peace under her maiden name and had a part-time job at a local wildlife park. Horace asked Marcus could he find out if Susan would be all right with a visit and a chat, so he could carry out Trevor's last wish. Susan agreed and Marcus said he would drive. They planned a catch up with the whole family the next day for a picnic at Parramatta Park. Susan was still a little scared about being found by the Rizky Lestari's network and didn't want her new address known. She would eventually ring Gladys, tell her story and ask her to destroy the letter.

Horace was back in his jeans and shirt the next day and Marcus picked him up early. As they drove to Parramatta, he commented on the growth of hi-rise accommodation in the suburbs and the expensive toll roads. When they arrived at the park, the sun was shining and everything was green and bright. Horace was amazed to see the changes around Parramatta Park. The last time he visited Parramatta it was just a suburban town. The heritage structures from the nineteenth century when the town stood as the Nation's crossroad of trade, had all but disappeared. Now, standing adjacent the World Heritage listed Old Government House, the vista was of a football stadium and glistening hi-rise. It all seemed to be overpowering the city's wonderful past.

Harry, Ruth and Susan arrived a short time later. Ruth had a basket of lunch treats and a thermos of coffee. She also bought a thermos of tea, thinking that might be the Englishman's preferred drink. Horace was very appreciative; they were a lovely couple. He asked Susan to have a quiet chat and stepped aside from the group. Susan agreed and then started to cry. She had been aware of Trevor's death and Horace consoled her:

"I'm sorry for your pain and fear Susan, there are ruthless people in the world, and whatever the reason, Trevor did not deserve to die like that. His last words were to give you this pouch and tell you he loved you. It contains a cross and a ring, it's all he had to give in his final minutes. I believe the police in Broome sent the cash he had left, to his mother. She told me to get you to call her sometime."

Susan hugged and thanked him for taking the time to come and see her. They went back to the group and enjoyed a pleasant lunch. Harry was a retired history buff now and told Horace all about Parramatta's recent struggles to save the local heritage, he said it was a losing battle. As Marcus and Horace drove back to Sydney, they talked about tragedy, life and humour. As he thanked Marcus and wished him and Sally a happy life, he offered up a Shakespearian quip from 'All's Well That Ends Well':

'The web of life is of a mingled yarn good and ill all mixed together.'

That night Horace had his Shakespearian fix at the Kirribilli Theatre. The laughter went a long way towards easing the recent traumatic events. The next morning, he headed off to Sydney airport, keen to catch up with Waiehu. The check-in nightmare was as per normal, but the weather was still great and talk of fires, floods and murders had faded.

CHAPTER 22...TAMING OF THE LION

The two remaining *'Lions of Mogadishu'*, Axmed and Zahi, had gone incognito. There was a nationwide warrant for their arrest. They had travelled separately in different transport modes and made their way to Melbourne. Somali refugees had settled in West Heidelberg in Victoria back in 1982 when their country's civil war forced millions to flee. The present population was in the thousands which made it a good place for the remaining two *'Lions of Mogadishu'* to hang out, until the Sydney drama settled down. Their cousin had an unused granny flat; it was the perfect hide out.

In Gaborone Botswana, Tebogo Modise had his Larona-pula network organise for the transfer of the water bottle with the diamond to the cutter and fence in New York. A local Somali teenager picked up the bottle from Zahi. The water bottle would be placed in the luggage of an unsuspecting young traveller heading to New York. The Somali lad was a deft hand at picking the right type of traveller with the right type of luggage and finding out their destination. In a friendly conversation he would offer the young traveller some advice and a ribbon to identify his luggage at the other end. That ribbon was coloured blue, black and white, the Botswanan flag colours. On arrival in New York two agents of Larona-pula would be waiting with the description of the traveller and his luggage. One would distract the traveller, while the other would grab the luggage from the baggage terminal remove the bottle and put the bag back on the conveyor.

All went as planned, and a month later Tebogo was informed that the cut diamond was valued at fourty million dollars. The buyer was happy, but only half of the offshore account funds came through. Tebogo was still enraged and contacted Zahi. He demanded he pursue the other water bottle or die trying, the larger stone could fetch fifty million. It had been two months since the death of Taifa and their police trail had gone cold. Tebogo decided to split the 'Lions' up. That may make their movements less detectable. Zahi was to go back to Lismore and Axmed to Nimbin. They were not happy about the new orders. Both men thought it was a useless mission but they lived in fear of Tebogo. They changed their appearance as best they could by growing beards and dressing down to grunge gear like vagrants.

Zahi once again studied the backpack taken from Pimple. It had been washed clean and appeared empty. He then noticed a small flap in the stitched corner of one of two zippered pockets. There was a folded piece of white cardboard wedged under the flap. He opened it up, it was faded from the dampness but still readable. It was a simple card with a picture of a Derby Bowler hat, the name Horace Winterbottom of 'Finding Earth Magazine,' and their Web address. Axmed and Zahi both looked at the card, "that's strange," said Axmed:

"I saw a bloke with a hat like that in Broome."

Zahi's mood suddenly changed:

"And I saw a bloke with a hat like that in Nimbin. It looks like we have a new path brother, and some phone calls to make. That funny hat fellow must be this Horace Winterbottom, and it can't be just a coincidence that he is always hanging around. He must know more."

When told about the added information Tebogo agreed that it was a good lead. He would make enquires on Horace Winterbottom of *'Finding Earth Magazine,'* from Gaborone, there was less chance of web tracing. Zahi was still to go to Lismore and Nimbin. Axmed was told to await further instructions.

Two days later Tebogo contacted Axmed and in his normal assertive voice gave the orders:

"This Horace fellow has gone back to England. The company would not give his address but from some old on-line magazine stories, we found out he lives in a village called Bourton-on-the-Water in the Cotswold. You are going there. Get a car, drive across to Two Rocks north of Perth, be there in six days. I will have a boat called the *'Mockingbird'* waiting for you, it will convey you to Mogadishu where you will be put on a flight to London. Your task is to find this Winterbottom and get some answers."

Then he hung up. The two remaining *'Lions of Mogadishu',* Axmed and Zahi, packed their gear, organised the cars, shook hands and went their separate ways.

* * *

Hekan Nabbu was still on the case. They knew from data traffic that the Africans were somewhere in Melbourne and suspected they would have people in the Somalian enclaves, and that they would give them cover. Dave Lang was back at work, his arm was healing well and his hand could once again grip a gun if needed. He and two other agents were watching the West Heidelberg area. Axmed was an unknown but the agents had an identikit photo of Zahi. Dave didn't need it; he had an image of this murderer fixed in his brain.

Axmed headed off to Perth in the car of a local Somalian friend, who would later report it as stolen. Zahi caught an Uber to an outer suburb to hot wire a car and start his journey north. A brief time later Dave Lang received a call from one of the agents that an African man matching the identikit photo, was just seen in an Uber heading towards La Trobe and he was following it. Dave and his team headed for the area. A S.W.A.T team was organised as a backup. Fifteen minutes later they had Zahi covered on three sides with the La Trobe University in front.

Zahi's Uber was on the outer La Trobe ring road and Zahi was still unaware that he was being followed. The Uber driver dropped him off at a carpark and continued down the road. Zahi had a choice of cars here. Dave Lang now had him cornered. Police and agents approached from north and south. Zahi was checking out the cars when he spotted the police units, he realised his predicament and headed for a path opposite the car park. He ran down the path and the officers gave chase. He emerged near the Human Resources unit and the S.W.A.T team appeared on the road to his right. He would not go down easy, he thought of himself as a proud lion.

A student was getting out of her car near a recycling box, Zahi grabbed her as a hostage and stood with his back to the box. His Bowie knife was on her throat when the officers arrived. Dave Lang took control of the situation and ordered that they regroup in the car park.

He dispersed the S.W.A.T team around the area and had a sniper positioned on the roof of an adjacent building. He then tried to talk to Zahi:

"Release the lady and lie face down on the ground, there is no way out of this situation."

Zahi had no fear and although the knife was on the girls throat, his mind was elsewhere. He had no intention of surrendering. The smell of the adjacent wet eucalypt forest and the sound of birds in the trees reminded him of the days he and his brothers hunted Impalas in the Chobe National Park.

Dave was watching Zahi closely; he was thinking of the lady's safety and that this killer may fight to the death. He decided to tell the sniper to take a shot when a chance arose. It was at that moment Zahi realised that the agent who had him cornered was the same person involved in Taifa's death. He became enraged and pointed the knife at Dave, the word 'you', was his last expression as the sniper's weapon discharged. Like his brother before him a bullet in the brain put another lion to death.

CHAPTER 23...THERE I SHALL END

Horace stayed a month at the flat with Waiehu catching up on his travel notes. Their relationship was getting stronger by the day, but he needed to return to England and submit his work. They talked of an Island holiday, but that would have to wait until he returned. It was then that Waiehu said she had finished one unit of her course and she could have a month off:

"Why don't we both go to England, I would love to meet your Mum."

They had a send-off dinner with the Couche's on the night before the flight. Esmeralda cooked up a tasty Ukrainian stew. The next morning Isiah dropped them off at Brisbane Airport. The flight would take a grueling twenty-six hours, with a quick stopover in Singapore. Flying didn't bother Waiehu but Horace hated it. He was full of travel anxieties.

When he was younger, Horace suffered from control anxiety. He reasoned that on a train or in a boat he had some control to save his life if there was an incident, but on a plane, it was all up to the pilot. Later in life, around the 911 terrorist atrocities, he suffered from racial anxiety. Every person with a goatee beard was eyeballed for the entire flight. All that was behind him now, these days it's just comfort anxiety. Thankfully, 'Finding Earth Magazine' pays for premium economy. That's only six inches of extra leg comfort and slightly better prepackaged food.

Australia, being so far away from the rest of the world means that every time you hop on an airplane, you must go back to the nineteenth century of privileged snobbery and suffer the long agonising pain of *'Cattle Class'* flights. The *'Class Compactor'* design in the seat configuration, means the tiny people of the world are the only people who smile at the hostess when boarding the plane. Extremely large travelers, who are generally victims of western diets, need all their seat and half of their neighbors to accommodate their mass. Being smothered by someone else's body is not a pleasant experience. The next day after you arrive, the hours of discomfort start to fade and you no longer feel like a sardine. That's when the planes air-conditioned circulated viruses start to eat away at your immune system.

Horace was in luck this time around; they shared two seats by the window with no Mr. Squeezy. He managed to sleep for at least an hour, spoke to Waiehu about his father and mother, and drank his allotted share of alcohol while his lady snoozed.

Horace's father, Harold spent the last ten years of his military career in the Royal Household Cavalry. He passed away at the age of 65 years from a heart attack and was duly honored. One room in the present Winterbottom home in Bourton-on-the-Water was resplendent in memorabilia from Harold's days in the saddle. The Queen herself had presented Harold a gift for his exemplary service. It was a hand-woven Afghan rug. It now took the winter chill out of the floorboards in Horace's room. Harold's trooper's sword took pride of place above the fireplace mantle. Florence was proud of her husband's service and kept that sword in pristine condition. It was a talking piece for visitors, as was the rug. She would espouse his virtues at every opportunity. Florence herself served in the military as a nurse, she was a tough lady. Horace was their only child and a late arrival. He was not of the military ilk; in fact, he detested war and all its shortcomings. He was far less Tory than his parents and believed reason and diplomacy could solve most issues. Of late though, with the autocratic regimes of Russia and China, he was starting to have thoughts, that with human frailty and greed, war may be inevitable.

After the nightmare run through Heathrow customs, Horace and Waiehu hired a car. Two hours later they approached Bourton-on-the-Water. Waiehu was enchanted. Spring was in the air and blossoms were sprouting in the hanging street baskets. Horace loved his hometown and its wonderful golden sandstone dwellings. As they drove slowly through the village towards his home off Lansdowne Road, he pointed out places and told Waiehu some of his memories of growing up there. They eventually pulled up out the front of Horace's home. It was a modest three bedroom double storey building. But Waiehu could see by the enthusiasm on Horace's face it was more than just a house, it was his home. The 'Noddy and Big Ears' garden box, and the ceramic 'Wind in the Willows' characters in the front yard, gave testament to that.

They knocked and walked in the open front door of his home. His mother Florence was there waiting and alive with welcoming excitement. She hugged Horace and gracefully shook the Japanese lady's hand. It would take a while for a lifetime of war prejudices to fade. Horace was a tiny bit nervous:

"This is my friend Waiehu, mum."

Florence gave a curt smile and welcomed her, if Horace was happy, she was.

The neighbor Beryl, who had fancied Horace, would be less enthused. She went to visit her sister Mabel in Manchester when she heard that Horace was coming home with his new Japanese girlfriend. The first thing Florence said to Waiehu before offering tea and biscuits was:

"You must come in and see Harold's sword and memorabilia room."

It was obvious to Waiehu that Florence missed her husband deeply.

They woke the next day, after a long jet-lagged sleep. Outside it was a cool Cotswold morning, but inside the central heating was keeping the home at a pleasant temperature. Horace's room was on the ground floor facing the street, which had very little traffic in the morning. Waiehu was snuggled up to Horace under the doona and listening to morning songbirds, she was feeling content.

Horace was also in a love inspired good mood. It was only dampened by the onset of a head cold, most likely complements from the planes circulated viruses. His eyes scanned the shelves in his room looking at the stories behind his Australian trinkets. Gus Cook's Blue Swimmer crab mounted on a piece of a Jarrah tree had him thinking about Chilli Jam Johnson and his dog Speed. He looked at the boomerang that had sent him flying for cover, the shark tooth that brought back the memory of Ajax's arm and the soft Quokka toy that reminded him of the Hucksters. Then there was the stone axe, and he remembered those two rude Asian fellows in Kojonup, who had some involvement in Trevor Trussells sad death. He then focused on the koala piggy bank from Nelson Bay and remembered the excitement of finding Kyle alive. Next to the koala piggy bank stood the fancy water bottle that cost him ten dollars. Horace was still unaware that a $50 million diamond sat in the base of that bottle.

He suddenly had a Shakespearian thought. When Demetrius spoke to Helena in a *'Midsummer night's dream'*, he said:

'I am sick when I do look on thee.'

That's how Horace now felt when gazing at that innocuous container, there was more to the story and he would eventually get to the bottom of it.

✱ ✱ ✱

Axmed arrived at Heathrow airport in London and heard a news reporter talking of a shooting death of a Somalian National in West Heidelberg Victoria:

'A knife was held to the throat of a lady at Latrobe, after a car chase and a kidnapping, police had no choice but to shoot the offender.'

Axmed had a deep sense that he had lost another brother, his anger flared. He now wanted some form of retribution. At this stage all he could do was complete the mission and hopefully find some answers. He went through customs on his Botswanan passport with no issues. Dressed in a stylish suit, he looked like just another businessman on a mission. The haircut and a neatly trimmed beard added to his charade.

Axmed retrieved his bag at the terminal and made

his way to the amenities block. He placed his knife and scabbard in a body holster under his shirt. Customs would be concerned with a concealed gun, but a knife in a bag in the belly of a plane offered no harm. Catching a cab was the easy part, finding a driver happy for a two-hour fare to Bourton-on-the-Water was harder. He found a willing driver but had to pay him for his return journey. Axmed didn't care and to the driver, a four-hour trip to the country and back would be a bonus.

Axmed was dropped off near the main park in Bourton-on-the-Water, this was a tourist village, and an African was just another tourist. He did what all new visitors do, he walked the street and browsed the shops, getting a sense of the environment. A hotel room not far from the post office, with a view of the main street was acquired. It was a perfect place for a stake-out. There were only a few men in bowler hats around, but Axmed knew the face he was looking for; the Broome incident was etched in his mind. It was only three days later when he spied his prey while having breakfast at the hotel.

Horace and Waiehu had just finished their morning tea at the Windrush Café. They had walked from the house to the café, and now Horace had some business to do at the Post Office. Waiehu took the opportunity to do some window shopping at the various tourist trinket businesses. Horace was in his civilian dress, jeans and a long sleeve shirt, but he still wore the bowler hat, it was his distinguishing feature both here and abroad.

Axmed spotted his prey, at first he wasn't sure this English gent seemed thinner. He remained out of site near an open window at the hotel and listened. There was not a lot of passing traffic and he could hear people talking. Horace came out of the Post Office at the same time Waiehu exited a shop and she called out his name, to get his attention. Axmed then smiled, he had his mark. He followed them to the house, keeping well out of view, he now had a location to conduct an interrogation, he would return after sundown.

A cool breeze was coming from the east along the Windrush River as Axmed walked towards Florence's house. It was a moonless night; the dull scattered streetlamps offered minimal light. There were lights on in the downstairs section of Florence's house as he approached. He kept in the dark, adjacent to some shrubs and headed to the corner of the building. Axmed stalled momentarily when his knee hit the Noddy garden box. He remained silent and ignored the pain, then listened by the window to three people talking. It was a bedroom; an older lady was at the door and the hat man and a woman were sitting on a bed. He looked around the room and smiled at what he could see. An interrogation wouldn't be necessary now, the water bottle he was after was on a shelf next to an Australian boomerang. It was a collection of memorabilia, most likely from the hat man's trip. He could grab the bottle when they slept and flee with no fuss, this surely will please Tebogo Modise. He was thinking of his brothers and pondered on killing this family to appease his anger at the loss of his own family. He wasn't sure that it would be a wise choice.

It was 2:00am when Axmed returned, he had with him a torch and his beloved Bowie knife, he was still considering using it. He forced the front door open without much effort, deadlocks and door alarms were for city folks. He stopped and listened, all was quiet. He then proceeded to make his way to Horace's room, being careful, because the floorboards tended to creak a little.

Florence was a light sleeper; she had been ever since Harold died. A noise stirred her, and she laid there listening. Axmed entered Horace's room, he had the fine beam of the torch pointing at the water bottle. As he grabbed it, he bumped the boomerang, it fell to the floor with a thud. Both Horace and Waiehu woke immediately. From the dim light of the outside streetlamps, they viewed a large dark man holding the water bottle and a torch in one hand, and a large Bowie knife in the other. Horace and Waiehu both froze in shock for a moment as did Axmed. Then suddenly Waiehu launched across the bed and karate kicked the African's hand, the knife flew across the room. Horace jumped up, snatched up the stone axe head from the shelf and threw it at the African. It hit him on the nose. This enraged Axmed, he dropped the bottle and the torch and grabbed Horace by the neck in a strangle hold. Horace was gagging but the green belt in judo finally came in handy. He remembered the move to off balance his opponent, and Axmed had to let go of one hand. While this was happening Waiehu grabbed the koala piggy bank and smashed it on the back of the Africans head, it barely dazed him, he shoved her against the window. Horace was then thrown down on the rug like a rag doll, Axmed was in a rage, he clutched the knife near the door, he then turned to face Horace again. All the Englishman's past horrors came back to haunt him. This was the same brute who killed Trevor Trussell. He suddenly had an attack of Déjà vu, but Mozzy wasn't here to save him this time. This large African killer was about to plunge a Bowie knife into Mr funny-hat's chest. Horace thought all was lost, when suddenly the sharp tip of his father's Trooper's sword appeared to come from within the heart of Axmed. The last 'Lion of Mogadishu' fell to the floor with a death stare of hate and a copious amount of his blood pouring over the Afghan rug. The Queen would not be pleased. Florence stood there at the door in her nighty, shaking her head. Her words, in true English fashion, helped nullify the situation:

"Now, what's all this fuss about Horace, who is this beast?"

The three stood there in stunned silence for a minute, then Florence went to ring the police. Waiehu sat back on the bed and Horace grabbed the water bottle, sat down, and cuddled her:

"I thought there was something special about this water bottle, my guess is it holds a diamond, and when were you going to tell me about your Karate skills?"

CHAPTER 24...TILL BE MORROW

The dramas of the previous day held sway for a week. It was all talked through, and the police performed their duty of care. Hekan Nabbu was summoned from Australia to add some light to the history that preceded the attempted robbery and the subsequent death of the African Axmed. He met with Horace once again and thanked him for his involvement in the case:

"We have had some break throughs with these criminal syndicates Horace. There is a new President in Botswana following elections there, and the diamond will be returned to the country. It was hinted that you may even be in for a reward."

Horace didn't hold out much hope for that. If it did come to pass, he had some thoughts on how to spend it.:

'A donation to the Lismore flood appeal, and a big party back in Australia with all his new friends. Perhaps an engagement party.'

Hekan also informed him that there had been a flurry of dealings in the weeks leading up to Axmed's death. Interpol had encouraged political forces within the Botswana and Indonesian governments to investigate their respective criminal organisations. The Larona-pula syndicate, Tebogo Modise and Rizky Lestari, were all now on criminal watch lists in their countries. As were the corrupt officials who helped sponsor them. The new Botswanan President said that the sale of the diamond from the water bottle will help finance the exposure and prosecution of these syndicates.

Over the following weeks Horace and Waiehu rekindled their holiday spirit and had some pleasant country outings and visits to heritage estates. Florence had the Afghan rug steam cleaned and she scrubbed and polished the Troopers sword when the police returned it. She placed it back above the fireplace and all things returned to normal. Horace was asked if he wanted the Bowie knife as a token of the traumatic event. He accepted it and placed it on his travel shelf. His thoughts were of Macbeth:

'Is this a dagger which I see before me, the handle towards my hand? Come, let me clutch thee.'

Plans were made for Waiehu's return to Australia and Horace was already missing her at the thought. 'One Earth' were pleased with his submissions from the Australian adventure and a new project was on offer. Subscriptions were on the increase and stories from the Southern Hemisphere were very popular in Europe. The company now had plans to open an office in Brisbane and informed Horace that there was an opportunity for him to work out of there. He was naturally thrilled and accepted straight away. The days of being a home lad, living with his mother had come to an end. He didn't rush to tell Waiehu, he wanted to ask her something first.

Horace, although smitten by the Bard was not the overly romantic type. He realised that he loved Waiehu and was prepared at last to commit. The family jeweller in the village had provided Horace with a beautiful diamond ring to help display that love. He wasn't sure if Waiehu felt as deeply as he did about their relationship but he was about to find out. He planned a day out at the local Bird Park and Jurassic dinosaur display. He knew how much Waiehu loved animals and history.

The sun was out and the Windrush River sparkled with reflective diamonds as they walked to the park. After a look around the aviary, then a wonderful lunch, they found themselves alone in a treescape with replica tyrannosaurs, sauropods and oviraptors of various shapes and sizes. Waiehu was pointing at and naming them, she was so happy. Horace grabbed her attention, he took her by the hand and chivalrously went down on one knee. Then quoting verbatim from Shakespeare's Midsummers Night Dream:

"Waiehu," *'I wooed thee with my sword and won thy love, doing thee injuries; But I will wed thee in another key, with pomp, with triumph and with reveling.'* "Will you consider marrying a Bowler wearing Englishman such as I?"

Waiehu's eyes widened in amazement, her smile would melt a glacier and she kissed him:

"I will, I will Horace, you are the man I love, you are my Theseus."

The End

(C... Parting is such sweet sorrow.
Remember love is a currency spend it wisely.)

MEMORIES FROM HORACE'S VINTAGE SCHOOL CASE

Ceramic Koala Bear piggy bank from Lavender Bay, exchanged for Boomerang.

Botticelli's Venus print from Broken Hill.

Dream-time serpent painted boomerang from Kalgoorlie

White Pointer shark tooth from Gracetown.

A small plastic Blue Swimmer Crab, mounted on a piece of a Jarrah tree, with a message:

'Enjoy your crabby time in Augusta'.

A small Quokka soft toy from Walpole.

Book on the Light-Horsemen from Albany.

An imitation stone axe head from Kojonup.

Monogrammed beer coolers, from Monkey Mia of dolphins and ancient stromatolites, and various pub coasters from all over Australia.

An artwork from Arnhem Land of a dreamtime serpent carving the local rocky canyons.

The Hucksters, very special drink bottle.

A replacement Koala Bear piggy bank from Nelson Bay, stating:

'Koala's were once plentiful around Port Stephens; we now need to protect them'.

BOOKS BY THIS AUTHOR

About That Shout. The History Of Parramatta Pubs And Inns

Historical -
The history of Pubs in Parramatta from 1800 to 1900
ISBN: 978-0-9953680-0-2

The Cull - Resolution Pending

Science Fiction-
ISBN: 978-0-9953680-3-3
From the pristine waters off Tasmania, to the streets of multicultural Parramatta, in a world now battered by climate change and the Covid-19 pandemic, we are challenged to face the inevitable. Marlin Jackson a boy prodigy receives a message from a fifth dimensional life form called the MUZE. Their time is non-linear, as infinite as the size of our universe, and at a right angle to our perception abilities. With their help Jackson may find an answer, but we are a resource driven species destined for extinction and we are eight billion too many. Their invitation has been sent, acceptance is pending, and it is not negotiable.

Where Eels Lie Down - A Parramatta Tale

Historical fiction-
ISBN: 978-0-9953680-4-0
From convict beginnings and Aboriginal interactions to the multinational and cultural diversity of today, the residents of Parramatta go about their lives. Stories

intertwine in a soup bowl of dysfunctional relationships. The lake is far from being a safe place; murder, fear and cruelty have found a footing. Normal people are caught up in the realities of life. The common place for soul searching and relaxation is the lake, with its tranquil water and peaceful walks. It is a haven for good and evil. This colloquial yarn with a 'boys-own' twist is a tale that melds the nature of heroes, villains and a giant lake bound eel. The settings for this novel are the Lake Reserve, a local pub, and the streets of Parramatta. They blend history, local issues, and 'Dreamtime' mysticism. This is all mixed with the life and love of a man and woman, whose feelings are woven by nature within: 'The Place Where Eels Lie Down'.

From Cradle To Covid- My Three Score And Ten

Autobiography-
A life in Western Sydney.
ISBN: 978-0-9953680-6-4
The original concept of this book was to create a family bible or an autobiography about the life and thoughts of a Sydney suburban layman philosopher. The word Philosophy is derived from Ancient Greek, it means for the love of wisdom. It is a way of thinking about the world, the universe, and society. All the things that have made me tick for seventy years. This was to be my story for now and reference into the future. I had the thought that in two hundred years a descendant could read what it was like to live through my time. Then between 2019 to 2021 we were incarcerated in lockdowns, which highlighted the one thing us Australians have always

taken for granted, our freedom.

ABOUT THE AUTHOR

Gary John Carter

Luck was on my side, to be born in Australia in 1952, it was akin to winning the biggest lottery in the world. The World Wars were over, I was a baby boomer and I had it all in front. I would be lucky enough to miss out on the Vietnam War. I would see man walk on the moon, the creation of transistors, silicon chips and a digital world. I would listen to the best music ever written, by some of the best musicians ever born.

I have an Electrical Trades background worked in the Electrical supply industry for over 40 years. My family has had a connection with Parramatta since about 1800. I have lived a basic Sydney suburban life and avoided the stepping-stones of strife. I planted a few trees as my houses turned to homes. I had a son and a daughter with the help of a wife, and I have authored a few books in my life. I am also blessed with grandchildren.

The self is just a droplet in the ocean of others, and only one lonely leaf in a forest. The only way to be remembered is to leave behind a droplet of inspiration, a leaf of thought or a written memory of both. As my days are now getting faster, I am grateful for the cause and effect granted by the 'The Big Bangs' master.

www.ingramcontent.com/pod-product-compliance
Lightning Source LLC
Chambersburg PA
CBHW060550260626
47161CB00003B/1134